"What about me?" Sasha asked.

Nick's grin was slow and sensual as he moved in on her so close she could feel the heat of his breath on her face. "Run a couple of tricks by me, gorgeous."

Telling herself she was not being stupid remaining alone with a man who came from a crime family, Sasha began to circle him, allowing her body to flow naturally. His gaze on her was cloying and potent. In unwanted response, her breasts tightened beneath the thin material, and heat crawled up her inner thighs. She felt as if his hands were all over her, when he wasn't even touching her...making love to her, when all he was doing was evaluating her as a potential show girl.

As long as his hands stayed where they were, she'd play along. And if not...she knew how to take care of herself with wise guys. She'd been forced to learn.

ABOUT THE AUTHOR

Friends often note that if it sparkles, Patricia Rosemoor will wear it. And what town has more sparkle than Las Vegas? She found the research highly entertaining, from the wedding chapels to the nightly shows. But it was the town itself that wowed her. Where else could she see a pyramid and sphinx with a laser-light show, a castle, a golden lion, a Roman forum, an exploding volcano and a pirate fight, all in one night? Patricia hopes you'll enjoy your vicarious visit to the most outrageous city in the world.

Books by Patricia Rosemoor

Drop Dead Gorgeous
Patricia Rosemoor

Harlequin Books

TORONTO • NEW YORK • LONDON
AMSTERDAM • PARIS • SYDNEY • HAMBURG
STOCKHOLM • ATHENS • TOKYO • MILAN
MADRID • WARSAW • BUDAPEST • AUCKLAND

To my mother-in-law, Florence Majeski, for always being so supportive and reading everything I write.

Thanks to Kim Daskas, Publicity Co-ordinator of the Luxor Hotel, and to Little Chapel of Flowers for making my research a pleasure.

ISBN 0-373-22317-X

DROP DEAD GORGEOUS

Copyright © 1995 by Patricia Pinianski

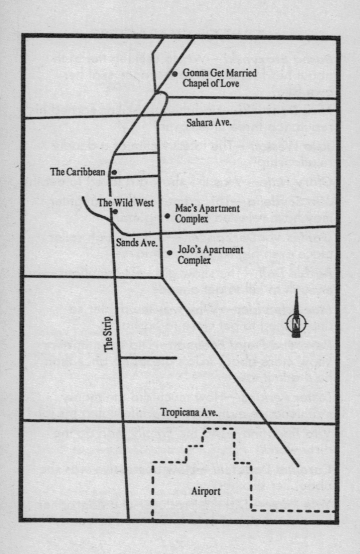

CAST OF CHARACTERS

Sasha Brozynski—Would seeking the truth about her friend's disappearance seal her own fate?

Nick Donatelli—Had the lady-killer earned his reputation three times over?

JoJo Weston—The latest victim of a deadly relationship?

Glory Hale—Was the show girl loved to death?

Mia Scudella—This crime family's daughter may have rejected the wrong man.

Gaines VanDerZanden—Did the high roller place even higher stakes on love?

Barbie Doll—The show girl was ambitious—but enough to kill to get ahead?

Mac Schneider—Why was the dealer so determined to get close to Sasha?

Reverend Floyd Edelman—Did the minister know more about JoJo's disappearance than he'd admit to?

Lester Perkins—How much did the mousy maintenance man observe while doing his job?

Vito Tolentino—Did the *Family* man do the dirty work?

Caroline Donatelli—How possessive was she about her brother?

Yale Riker—Did the producer-choreographer have some secret JoJo threatened to betray?

Prologue

Las Vegas. A neon harlot with a greedy heart.

Myriad colors flashed up and down the strip in overload. When she'd seen it for the first time, she'd been overwhelmed, as were the tourists still scavenging the streets in the middle of the night, searching for the slot machines or the crap table with the best odds. Now she knew different. Everything here was an illusion, nothing more than expensive plastic.

And just about everyone had a con in this town where excess was the norm.

Now she knew you kept paying and paying and paying, if not in cash, then with your very soul.

The doors behind her swished open, allowing the various tones of the innumerable slot machines strung across the casino to drift toward her. Sometimes she heard in her sleep the bizarre musical cadence they created. Luckily, she didn't have to work in the pit or she would lose her mind.

She might lose it, anyway.

What was she going to do?

Not about her car that had just refused to start, and after she'd had a new battery installed. But about the other, the thing that was racking her conscience. She was in a moral dilemma. How could she know and not tell?

She thought to take a taxi home, but she didn't live far, barely a mile, and a walk might clear her mind. Give her time to make a decision. Shouldering her bag that contained her personal stage makeup and hairpieces, she set off south down the strip, already considering her options. She could keep what she'd learned to herself and stay safe. Or she could talk and chance the outcome.

How bad could the consequences be? she wondered. The police would protect her, wouldn't they?

She automatically turned east when she came to the construction site. The shortcut would get her home faster. The old hotel-casino was closed for the season while it got a face-lift and a new identity. Plenty of that going around in this town, she thought.

Sweeping along the construction site, she ventured into deserted territory. The backside of a casino on her left, chain-link fencing and boarding on her right. A few scattered work lights lit her way. Beyond the shadowy expanse lay a tract of low-income housing the typical tourist never saw—rows of two-story apartment buildings, many shoddy, home to the behind-the-scenes workers of the glamorous settings. Here the kitchen help and housekeeping menials found cheap residences within walking distance of their jobs.

Her job—maybe she should leave it, get someplace safe, then tell.

But where was safe? Should she really risk her skin?

Deep in thought, she was unaware of another presence until a scuffle echoed through the desolate urban canyon. Heart lurching, she glanced over her shoulder, saw the dark figure fast descending upon her. A mugger? Or another worker taking the shortcut home? Not wanting to take any chances, she gauged the distance between them, then ran for all she was worth.

Over the drumming in her ears, she heard leather slap pavement. Though the sound came from behind her, it quickly drew closer and echoed around her like mocking laughter, telling her she wasn't going to get away.

Desperate, she looked for a hiding place.

The construction site.

Spotting a break in the chain link fence, she squeezed through. Not fast enough. Her body jerked when a hand grabbed hold of her bag's strap. She was almost relieved as she disengaged from the thing, choosing to let the dark-clothed person have the makeup and hairpieces and the few bucks left in her wallet till payday.

"Go ahead, take it," she said, breath heaving, backing into the secluded construction area.

"It's you I want."

Recognizing the voice in the dark, she went cold inside. Her legs suddenly became stiff and awkward. She'd known. She'd been hoping...but she'd known.

"Don't do this. You don't have to do this," she insisted, hoping she sounded convincing enough. Dear Lord, she'd waited too long to make up her mind. Doing so on the spot, she promised, "I won't tell."

"I know you won't" came the taunting reply.

And though she couldn't see the face, the knife was hard to miss. Catching the glow of a nearby work light, the blade gleamed with deadly intensity as it slashed down toward her....

Chapter One

Las Vegas. What a kick!

The first thing Sasha Brozynski noted as she drove her rental car down Tropicana Avenue toward the Strip was an honest-to-God Egyptian pyramid fronted by a sphinx and obelisk that, in fact, comprised one of Vegas's newest and splashiest hotel complexes. On opposite corners stood a multitowered castle and a giant golden lion, heralding two other mega-hotels.

Like JoJo told her, everything in Las Vegas was bigger and more outrageous than anywhere else.

Knowing that, as a dyed-in-the-wool, born-and-bred New Yorker, she shouldn't be too impressed, Sasha decided that she didn't have to share her opinion with anyone. She could just secretly enjoy.

Her cheerful grin quickly faded, however, once she turned north onto Las Vegas Boulevard—a sea of cars stretching before her as far as the eye could see. Traffic was stop-and-crawl and, from the car rental company's map, she figured she had about four miles to go.

A glance at the car clock told Sasha she had less than twenty minutes to get to the wedding chapel where her best friend and former roommate, JoJo Weston, was about to be married. And she was the maid of honor.

She hadn't meant to cut her arrival this close, but JoJo hadn't called with the astounding news until two nights ago. Sasha hadn't been able to get out of New York until this morning, and then her flight had been delayed.

"C'mon, move it! Doesn't anyone in this town know how to move it? Sunday drivers!"

She punctuated her frustration with a blow to her horn.

Other horns blared back.

"All right, already," she muttered, slinking down into the seat. "I get the message."

The message being, she was going to be late and JoJo would kill her...just as she'd threatened to do on several other occasions over the dozen years they'd known each other. Somehow, Sasha's time clock habitually managed to be off a bit—perhaps her unconscious effort to counter the daily stresses she had to contend with living in New York City and working as a Broadway gypsy.

But this was not her fault. She'd really meant to be punctual today.

Really!

Sitting at a red light, she checked herself over in the rearview mirror. Darn! Though she'd changed into a new little silk number and had touched up her makeup shortly before the plane landed, her hair was a mess from the wind and her lipstick was practically nonexistent.

Determined to arrive looking her best, she pulled a wide-tooth comb from her purse and worked on the tangle of curls until the mass was sculpted around her face and shoulders rather than looking like something out of the blender. The light changed to green. Inching the car forward, she fumbled through her bag for her liner pencil and lipstick, waiting to use them until she hit the next red light a few moments later.

Then she was moving again, but the car's clock glared at her, giving her less than seven minutes to go.

"Oh Lord, JoJo, I'm sorry!"

She scanned the street for an address of some kind, her gaze skipping over the Strip's older glitzy hotels, including the Caribbean where JoJo worked in the showroom. She caught sight of a wedding chapel. Her spirits soared until she spotted the sign with the name. Wrong chapel. Las Vegas was famous for them. Barely a block later, she was disappointed again.

Four minutes and counting and another wrong chapel, this one looking more like a funeral home than a place to get married, Sasha thought with a shiver.

At least traffic was moving. With two minutes to go, she finally spotted the Gonna Get Married Chapel of Love—obviously named after the sixties pop tune—a tiny white building with a slanted roof and steeple.

Heartbeat settling into something near normal, she pulled into the almost empty parking lot. Triumphant that she'd made it in the nick of time, she was out of the car and running. And as she approached the entrance with no minutes to spare, she calmed herself and glided inside. No one stood in the small foyer, filled with photos of celebrities that had been married there, so she entered the chapel itself.

Interior walls, flooring and slanted ceiling were of raw wood. White-satin bows and silk flowers decorated rows of bench seating. Silk trees decked with Italian lights and white doves and electric candelabra on floor stands lined the front of the chapel. To her right was an organ. To her left, a bower of silk greenery and flowers, obviously meant to be a setting where a photographer could take formal shots of the bride and groom.

Only there was no photographer... no organist... no minister.

No bride or groom!

"What's going on?"

"Can I help you?" came a thready voice.

Sasha turned so fast she almost fell off her platform sandals. Before her stood a sixtyish-looking man with thinning salt-and-pepper hair. He was a little shorter than she, but many men were, even when she wasn't wearing heels. His slight frame was encased in a long purple robe, so she assumed he was the minister.

"I'm here for a wedding. JoJo Weston. Did I get the day or time wrong?"

"No, but perhaps she did," the minister said, censure in his tone. "Miss Weston was to have been here half an hour ago to prepare herself in our bride's room."

"You mean she's late for her own wedding?" Relieved, Sasha laughed. And here she'd been close to getting an ulcer over being late herself.

"Unfortunately, there will be no wedding." The minister started to turn away.

"Excuse me, uh, Reverend...?"

He stopped and answered, "Floyd Edelman."

"Reverend Edelman, why no wedding?"

"Because I have another couple booked in half an hour. Since your friend is not yet here, I don't believe there will be sufficient time to complete the ceremony."

Good Lord, what a time for JoJo to pick up *her* bad habits. "Can I use your phone to call her?"

"I already did so. No answer."

"Then she's on her way," Sasha insisted. "She'll be here, and surely you can make time."

"Only if she shows up very soon."

"What about calling the groom?"

Reverend Edelman looked away. "Unfortunately, I don't have any information about him."

"He's probably listed. What's his name?"

"I couldn't tell you." His thin voice became strident.

"Wait a cotton-pickin' minute. You don't know who you're supposed to be marrying?"

Not that she had reason to criticize. JoJo had gotten off the phone so fast the other night, Sasha hadn't had a chance to ask for little details—like the full name of the prospective groom. JoJo had merely referred to the love of her life as *the Hunkman.*

"This whole affair has been slightly unusual," the minister was saying tersely. "I only met with Miss Weston two nights ago. She was very secretive." He fidgeted, twitched and looked downright disturbed. "She said she would arrange for the license. She booked the space, my services and that of the organist and photographer—they're in the lounge, unpaid for their time, as am I."

Now he was looking at her as if she might help correct that situation. A minister he might be, but he was also a businessman, and Sasha had been around too long to believe that Reverend Floyd Edelman would have booked the chapel and related services without a deposit.

"JoJo's probably caught in the darn traffic on the Strip. You don't mind if I wait here, do you?" she asked.

"Suit yourself."

His barely gracious words were backed by the sound of a car arriving.

Sasha took a relieved breath. "There she is now!"

But the arrival turned out to be the bride of the next wedding. As Reverend Edelman ushered the flustered young woman and her two companions toward the back to the bride's room, Sasha sank into a funk.

Where in the world were JoJo and her mystery man?

She perched against the back of the rear bench to wait.

A few minutes later, another car arrived. A groom and his companions. JoJo's groom? Sasha was about to dash forward when the minister intervened, escorting the young men to the lounge.

More cars. Guests for the next wedding—all dressed up to look like famous movie stars. They gave *her* curious stares as they entered the chapel and took their seats. The organist followed and warmed up. At the front of the chapel, the photographer quickly set up a video camera.

Still no JoJo.

And Sasha was getting worried. Seriously worried. This wasn't like her friend, not at all. Maybe JoJo had simply changed her mind, decided that she was being too impulsive. Maybe she'd called the guests she could reach and had canceled. But JoJo wouldn't have let *her* hang like this, knowing she was coming all the way from the coast.

And she certainly would have called the minister....

"Something's wrong," she told Floyd Edelman, cornering him near the chapel door.

"Obviously. But I'm afraid I don't have time to worry about Miss Weston's state of mind, since another couple is waiting. I'll have to ask you to leave now. The next wedding will begin in a few minutes.''

''Yeah, sure.''

Ticked that a supposed man of God didn't seem overly concerned, Sasha strode out of the place and slid into her rental car. She whipped out the map and located the street south of the chapel where JoJo lived, hoping that her friend was actually home with an out-of-order phone or something.

Besides, Sasha had been invited to use the apartment for as long as she planned to stay in Las Vegas—between gigs, she'd thought about checking out the town for work like JoJo had been bugging her to do since she'd moved—so where else should she go? Her friend had been planning to leave town, anyway, for a short honeymoon, and then she was supposed to move in with the Hunkman.

Staying away from the Strip this time, Sasha arrived at the apartment complex in a few minutes. The place wasn't as nice as some she'd seen, not as bad as others. Though the half-dozen buildings were old two-story jobs with an outside second-floor landing, they were tidy and freshly painted, and the grounds surrounding the central swimming pool were lush with high desert greenery, both foliage and cacti.

Finding the right building, the one that happened to be most isolated from the rest, Sasha bounded up the stairs and found 2C. Her banging on the door was enough to wake the dead . . . but no one answered.

''Damn!''

What now?

Figuring her ex-roomie hadn't changed, she lifted the welcome mat. No key. Heart sinking, she checked the lamp next to the door. Nothing. Finally, she ran her hand along the top of the heavily draped picture window.

Her fingers found metal in the right shape.

"Gotcha."

She was inside in seconds.

If a little dull—few personal touches to pick up the neutral walls and furniture—the place was neat as a pin. Vintage JoJo. The woman had an obsession with organization, but Sasha didn't hold that against her. The main room was for both living and dining. She checked around. The tiny kitchen and bath were equally neat, as was the single bedroom.

No signs of an excited bride getting ready for her wedding. From the look of her apartment, one would think this was just another day, that JoJo had made her bed, done her dishes and gone off to work as usual.

But it felt all wrong.

Sasha trusted her instincts, and her intuition told her that her friend was in trouble.

She picked up the phone and dialed the police... and got exactly nowhere. No accident report for a JoJo Weston. When Sasha insisted that JoJo might be missing, that maybe someone should start looking for her, the person on the other end suggested she do just that. Considering the lady in question was supposed to be getting married, the impersonal voice suggested that she might have eloped. In any case, no official move would be made until the woman had been missing for forty-eight hours. Though if she wanted, a squad would be sent over to take her statement now.

Furious that they wouldn't start the search immediately, Sasha slammed the receiver down and reconnoitered. Okay. So it was up to her. She should first eliminate the possibility of JoJo having eloped, but how to do that?

Suitcases!

Surely no woman would elope without taking plenty of clothes.

Checking the closet, the first thing that met her gaze was a white dress encased in plastic. Sasha pulled it out. A pretty, if somewhat plain, calf-length number trimmed with only a handful of pearls. While it wasn't elaborately traditional, Sasha was certain this had been the intended wedding dress. Quick tears seared the back of her eyelids.

Back to the closet. Stored on a high shelf were a wheeled Pullman case, a dress bag and an overnight bag. It didn't look as if JoJo had planned on going anywhere.

So what next?

Her job. If JoJo hadn't left town, she would be at work. And if she wasn't, maybe someone there would have some clue as to where she'd disappeared to. Grabbing her purse and keys, Sasha slammed out of the apartment and made for her rental car, her destination the Caribbean.

A lump in her throat, worst-case scenario niggling at her subconscious, Sasha only hoped that even if JoJo Weston hadn't gotten married today, she would still have the opportunity to live happily ever after....

A SENSE OF PURPOSE driving her, Sasha felt better by the time she arrived at the Caribbean, an older hotel-casino that had been saved from the wrecker's ball by a man named Nick Donatelli. JoJo had described Nick in glowing terms, insisting he was a real hunk . . . but that, on the down side, he was also *connected*—his father being Salvatore Donatelli, head of a known crime family, and who'd served hard time.

Considering Las Vegas was trying to clean up its image, to become, as JoJo had put it, the Walt Disney World of gambling—offering vacations for the whole family down to the smallest child—the new owner's ancestry had been played down when the Caribbean had been restored and reopened.

Not that Sasha gave a fig about who or what Nick Donatelli was. The only thing that concerned her was finding JoJo.

She slid through the noisy casino that seemed to go on forever. No matter one's destination—restaurant, bar, shops, showroom—gambling was smack in the middle of everything. A few players who were looking for more than a win tried to come on to her, but street-savvy, she successfully ignored them and went her way without missing a beat.

But as she reached the heart of the casino, one man caught her attention long enough to distract her from her purpose. Surveying the establishment, he looked as if he owned it. Her stride slowed as she checked him out.

His island white suit and bold red-and-gold flowered shirt heightened both his tan and his incredible physique. He was tall. Really tall. Tall enough to make Sasha feel like she didn't have a thirty-two inseam. He had a thick mane of longish dark hair that was crisply cut around bold features, including a Roman nose. He was drop-dead gorgeous and would never be overlooked by any woman. When his intense gaze met hers briefly, she felt her pulse rush.

Then his attention was robbed by a bigger man, not as tall, certainly, but wide enough to fill a doorway. One look at him and Sasha shivered, frightening memories she'd recently buried trying to surface....

She quickly regained her equilibrium and continued through the casino, putting thoughts of the bulky man out of her mind. The other wasn't so easily forgotten. Irritated with herself that she'd been so distracted, she renewed her determination to find her old friend. She soon spotted the Island Showroom, and since it was still early, more than an hour before the first of two nightly performances, few people were around.

She approached the employee guarding the showroom entrance, a young man in a flower-print shirt and khaki trousers. All the employees of the hotel-casino seemed to be dressed in casual and colorful uniforms.

"Can I help you?" he asked, his arched brows and expression as he stared at her telling Sasha that he would be more than happy to do so.

She gave him an amicable smile. "I'm looking for JoJo Weston. One of the dancers."

"I know JoJo. You a friend of hers?"

"Her *best* friend."

"You're from New York, right?"

"Howdya guess?" As if she didn't know her accent placed her as effectively as a gaudily lit theater marquee. "JoJo and I were roommates. We worked together as dancers in several Broadway shows."

He was perusing the length of her legs. "I'll bet."

"So, can I go in and find her?"

"Uh, it's against the rules to let anyone backstage who isn't on my list."

She gave him a pleading expression she usually reserved for the stage. "But JoJo's expecting me."

Apparently properly affected, he shifted uncomfortably. "She didn't leave word—"

"Because I was late. I was supposed to meet her elsewhere. Please, can't I go in?"

"I guess it wouldn't hurt nothing."

"Thanks..." She looked at his name tag—Francis—and gave him a thousand-watt smile. "Franky."

The young man beamed and swung open the door for her. He pointed to the left. "Go down that way. There's the entrance to the dressing rooms."

Sasha wasted no time. She scooted through before he could change his mind and before anyone else saw her. Another employee might not be nearly as accommodating as Franky.

Heart pounding, she opened the backstage door. Performers were arriving, one pretty and perky young woman leading her straight to the show-girls' dressing room. Inside was a near riot as noisy dancers pulled on costumes, applied heavy stage makeup or fixed hairpieces or wigs to their heads.

Only one woman, a voluptuous gray-eyed blonde more composed than the others, noticed her standing in the doorway. Tying a belt around her satin wrapper, she asked, "Who are you?"

"Sasha Brozynski, a friend of JoJo Weston's. You wouldn't have seen her tonight?"

"Not tonight." She swiveled in her chair toward the mirror, where she seemed to be admiring herself. "Or last night, either."

"You have no idea of where she might be?"

"Sorry."

"Look, something's wrong," Sasha said urgently. "JoJo didn't show for her own wedding."

The blonde's gray eyes widened in the mirror. "Her what?" She swiftly swiveled toward Sasha.

"She was supposed to be getting married today."

"To who?"

Sasha sighed. "I was hoping you could tell me."

The blonde stood and shouted over the other raised voices. "Hey, any of you know JoJo was getting married?"

That stopped the room cold. A half-dozen dancers in various states of undress turned to stare at Sasha, as did the others at the mirrored counter.

"I didn't even know she was dating anyone," one said.

"Me neither."

"No wonder she wouldn't let me fix her up with a high roller last week," a third girl put in. "So she got married, huh? Maybe that'll cool Mr. D's jets over her not coming in last night."

"But she didn't actually get married," Sasha explained. "At least, not that I know of. I was supposed to be her maid of honor. She didn't even cancel with the chapel. She just didn't show."

"Maybe she eloped to Reno or something," the blonde suggested.

"Her suitcases are still in her closet."

Someone in the back of the room laughed and shouted, "How many clothes do you need for a honeymoon?"

That sent the others into a fit of laughter. They weren't taking her concern seriously. No one was. They hadn't even known JoJo was dating. But someone at the Caribbean had to know something. The problem was, how was she going to figure out who and what? She wasn't about to leave it alone. She wasn't about to leave Las Vegas until she found out what happened to her friend.

An idea came to her.

JoJo had made her promise she would at least check into the work situation while she was here....

"Yeah," Sasha said, forcing a smile to her lips. "You're probably right. She eloped to Reno or something. I hope she gets back soon, though. She was going to make some introductions. Try to get me work." She lit up as if she'd just thought of a spontaneous idea. "Say, any chance I could get a job here?"

"You a Broadway gypsy like JoJo?" the blonde asked, giving her a better once-over.

"That's how we got to know each other."

"So you can dance. But can you strut? And do you mind showing off a little flesh?"

"I've had to show some flesh before," Sasha stated, though JoJo had warned her some of the costumes were far skimpier than in the average Broadway musical.

She had also assured her the Caribbean was one of several hotels that went against tradition—the show girls didn't bare their breasts, not even for the late show.

"Talk to Mr. D," one of the other girls said. "He has to give his okay to every show girl personally, anyhow."

"By Mr. D, you mean Nick Donatelli?" Sasha asked.

"You got it, honey," another said. "And you're just his type."

The implication being that would help her get a job. Squirming inside, Sasha looked straight at the blonde, who was now wearing a displeased expression and asked, "So how do I get in to see Mr. Donatelli?"

"You ask me nice," a deep voice rumbled from behind her.

The hair at the nape of her neck stood on end even as she turned to face the voice's owner. He really did fill a doorway, there being barely enough room for his shoulders to slide through. She fought the woozy feeling that suddenly came over her. His bulk was familiar, but not the brown hair silvered at the temples or the eyes so dark they were almost black.

She had to stop letting the past spook her—she'd never seen this man before today.

He was no danger to her.

She tried out a smile, though it felt a bit flat. "Who is it I'm asking?"

"Name's Vito Tolentino." He held out a beefy hand. "Mr. D's right-hand man."

"Sasha Brozynski, New York City." Noting a bulge under his left arm as she shook hands, certain he was packing a piece, she tried to keep from staring. "I'm between musicals at the moment and I wouldn't mind trying a turn around your stage."

"Mmm." The sound was noncommittal as was Vito's expression. "I guess the boss could take a few minutes to try you out. C'mon, I'll set you up with him."

Hoping that his statement was more innocent than it sounded, Sasha reluctantly followed him out the door to hoots and shouts of luck from the show girls. In the hallway, she glanced back to see the blonde wedged at the door and staring after her, her gray eyes filled with malevolence.

Startled by the unexpected rancor, Sasha stumbled.

A beefy hand gripped her upper arm, making her nearly jump out of her skin. She regained her poise fast and was relieved when he let go.

Shrugging, she said, "Nerves."

"Sure hope you dance better 'n you walk," Vito muttered.

And Sasha hoped she wasn't letting her feet take her where she didn't belong.

NICK DONATELLI opened the door to his penthouse apartment to let in Mac Schneider, a blackjack dealer who'd been working for him for several months. Nick had noticed the man was always a little weird around him. At the moment, he seemed a bit stiff, almost uncomfortable.

"You sent for me, sir?"

Dispensing with formality, he said, "The name's Nick. And contrary to rumor, I don't execute staff members who get outta line."

That startled the poor sucker, who took a step back. "Can I ask what I did?"

"Nothing. That was supposed to be a joke."

But the man still wasn't relaxing. He stood at attention, and unless Nick was imagining things, Schneider was actually glaring at him, as if he had reason to be ticked. And, as had happened more than once, Nick got the distinct impression that the dealer had some reason to dislike him.

"Look, the pit bosses tell me you're sharp and personable with the customers. The reason I asked you up was to find out whether or not you'd be comfortable dealing poker for some high rollers coming in tomorrow night."

"Poker?" Schneider seemed more than subtly relieved. "No problem."

"Good." Nick perched on the back of one of the couches. "Game starts ten o'clock, presidential suite. I expect you to be there at eight to check everything out with Vito. I want our guests to be comfortable, well fed and watered so they don't have reason to be unhappy.

You need anything you don't see, you tell Vito and he'll arrange it. I'll arrange your replacement in the pit.''

"What about the regular dealer *I'm* replacing in the game? What happened to him?"

Nick lifted one eyebrow. "He's been unavoidably detained."

Again the hostile look. "Detained?"

"In the hospital."

"He had an accident?"

Tempted to string him along, confirm all the rumors he was certain the dealer had heard, Nick changed his mind and told him the simple truth. "Appendicitis."

"Oh."

Nick took his time, crossed to the windowed wall with its view of the neon Strip below. "You got any questions?"

"No."

"Then that's it."

Dismissed, Schneider nodded and turned to go. Just then the front door opened and Vito strolled in, followed by the stunning woman he'd noticed in the casino earlier. The dealer stared at her hard, and Nick didn't blame him.

In a town of professionally gorgeous women, this one stood a head above the rest. Literally. It wasn't her face—her features were interesting, but he'd seen more beautiful. He wasn't sure he'd seen longer legs, though, and that mane of tawny hair that added a few more inches looked real. Every inch of her looked real. Her simple gold silk dress could pass for a slip and didn't hide a thing.

His reaction to her was instant and painful arousal. She was bigger than life and acted as if she didn't know it. He figured that meant she had enough self-confidence to handle the fact easily.

At least, she did until her gaze swept past Schneider and settled on him. Then she faltered a tad, enough for him to pick up on her hesitancy, and her golden-brown eyes widened as they met his.

Nick was flattered.

"Mr. D, we got a potential show girl here," Vito said.

He grinned. "Do we?"

"Sasha Brozynski," she stated, sounding a little breathless.

Vito added, "I figure maybe she can save us some trouble."

Not that Nick had ever minded getting into a little trouble when a desirable woman was involved. And he'd never met one more desirable than this one.

But then Vito dropped the bomb. "Says she's a good friend of JoJo Weston's."

Chapter Two

Sasha could hardly believe Nick Donatelli and the hunk she'd been attracted to in the casino were one and the same man. As he moved from the windows toward her, his stride long and intent, she couldn't stop her reaction. Her pulse picked up and her breathing grew shallow. For a moment, the room narrowed to just the two of them....

And then he looked away, releasing her.

Relieved, she followed his gaze to the employee wearing a dealer's vest. The man was still standing there, staring. At her. His speculative expression gave her the oddest feeling. Then Nick snapped his fingers to get the man's attention. As if waking from a hypnotic daze, the dealer jerked and without a word hurried out of the room, slamming the door closed behind him.

And then *his* eyes were on her again, trapping Sasha in an elemental way.

"Vito, you can leave."

"Right, boss." Vito slipped away swiftly and silently for such a big man.

"What about me?"

Nick's grin was slow and sensual as he moved in on her so close she could feel the heat of his breath on her face. "Run a couple of tricks on me, gorgeous."

His audacity threw her. "What?"

"You know, as in prance around like a show girl so I can get a better idea of the whole view."

Relieved that he hadn't meant anything more by the request, Sasha nevertheless had to smother her irritation. "I don't prance."

Telling herself she was not being stupid remaining alone in a room with a man who came from a crime family, one who might have no scruples where she was concerned, Sasha circled Nick. She did it for JoJo. And she did it for herself—to prove that she could without turning into a puddle of anxiety. Therapy and some physical training had done that for her.

She moved smoothly, allowing her body to flow naturally. His gaze on her was cloying and potent. In unwanted response, her breasts tightened beneath the thin material, and heat crawled up her inner thighs. She felt as if his hands were all over her when he wasn't even touching her...making love to her when all he was doing was carefully inspecting the package she would be presenting to an audience.

And there she was, overly attracted and resenting it. Resenting him. This was supposed to be professional, not personal. But she figured as long as his hands stayed where they were, and he made no untoward demands on her, she would play along.

And if not...she knew how to take care of herself with wise guys. She'd been forced to learn.

Stopping directly in front of Nick, Sasha turned in place. Slowly. So he could get as good a look as he wanted. He stepped closer, his eyes brushing her breasts on the way up to her face. She tensed, ready to fend him off, if necessary.

But he stopped, with breathing room to spare, reached out and ran a thumb lightly along her jawline. The sensation quickly spread to all ports of call. Before she could react and remove his hand, however, he did so himself.

"Your jaw was clenched," he told her. "Not very attractive. You'll have to work on that."

Mouth dry, she forced out a response. "I'm surprised you noticed." Considering how much attention he'd been paying to the rest of her.

"Not much gets by me," he stated. "You'd do well to keep that in mind."

Which sounded as if he expected her to be around for a while. "So is that it?" Not wanting to appear overly eager, she hesitated asking directly if she was hired.

"Let's have a drink."

A demand rather than a request.

Nick indicated she should sit. Instead, she sauntered to the windows, watching his reflection to see what he would do. He barely took his eyes off her as he crossed to the black veneer bar. The room was a study in black and white. White carpeting and couches, tables in black veneer to match the bar. Only the artwork—paintings and sculptures—and a big vase of flowers on a table against the wall presented splashes of color around the room.

Very classy. And very expensive. The decor in this room alone was probably worth more than her parent's entire house in Queens.

And this was just one room of many. From the look of the layout when she'd left the elevator, she guessed his apartment took up one-fourth of the hotel's top floor.

"What's your pleasure?" Nick asked.

Still staring at the window, Sasha said, "Whatever you're having." She thought she caught a flash of white teeth reflected in the plate glass, but she couldn't be certain.

Trying to distract herself, she looked beyond the window, out to the street far below. The sun had set, yet Las Vegas was brighter than ever. Sasha vaguely wondered what electricity bills were like for the hotels in this town. It boggled the mind.

Nick suddenly asked, "So why do you want to work for me?"

A loaded question. She didn't want to work for him. She would like to run as fast and as far as she could to get away. He was trouble. Deep in her gut, she knew it. But she had to remember she was doing this for JoJo. For her friend, she would put up with Nick Donatelli's arrogance and the disconcerting awareness that stretched between them like a finely tuned instrument waiting to be played.

"JoJo had only good things to say about working at the Caribbean."

"Not about me?"

"She hardly mentioned you," Sasha said truthfully.

Moving closer than was comfortable, he handed her a drink and then clinked glasses. Following his example, she threw back a quantity of the liquor without testing it first. A blaze followed the alcohol down her throat.

"What is this stuff?" she asked with a gasp.

"Mescal." Though he kept a straight expression, his green eyes seemed to be laughing at her. "An old southwestern drink made from the agave plant."

"It's wretched." Shuddering, she set her half-filled glass on a nearby table. "It makes me think of gasoline."

"I take it you're expert on the taste of gasoline?" He laughed aloud, but the rumble died quickly, his grin replaced by a grimace. "You know your friend JoJo took a powder on us last night. No notice."

"So I heard."

"Did she have any idea you were coming?"

"She invited me."

"Then you've seen her?"

Sasha shook her head. "I only wish." She thought to elaborate, to tell Nick about the aborted wedding, but she figured he, too, would suggest JoJo and her intended had eloped. She didn't need to hear the reprise of that old song again.

"I haven't seen her in a couple of months," she admitted. "Since the show we both had been dancing in closed."

"She came to Las Vegas and came to work for me right after that. So what have you been doing? Did your new show close its doors so soon?"

"Actually, I quit the show last fall and haven't worked since." Anxious to end the interview that was starting to give her the heebie-jeebies, and not intending to explain herself, she demanded, "So, do I have a job, or what?"

"Or what," he echoed, taking another swig of the disgusting liquor. "My producer-choreographer, Yale Riker, will have something to say about it."

"I was told you handpicked your show girls."

"I do. But only from the ones who have some real talent as well as looks. You can audition for Yale tomorrow morning."

"But *you're* satisfied, right?"

"Not by a long shot, honey," he said, his full lips twitching. "But I can wait."

The statement hung over her head like the sharp blade of a guillotine. Was he saying that he needed to audition her in his bed, as well?

"Look, Mr. Donatelli—"

"Nick."

"I don't mind strutting my stuff for you, as long as it's on a stage. Got the picture?"

"Oh, I got it, all right." He moved closer, his expression challenging, though she held her ground. "But you'll change your mind..."

He left the statement hanging. Might as well have added, *They all do.*

The liquor's fumes rushing out of her nostrils, feeling as if she were breathing fire, Sasha told him, "Hell will freeze over first." A stupid thing to say when her goal was to find out what happened to JoJo, especially considering she didn't have a shot from the outside. Now he'd probably throw her out on her fanny and then where would she be?

But he seemed amused, arrogantly saying, "Never make promises you can't keep."

NICK WAS SURPRISED when Sasha didn't challenge him again. She probably wanted to spit in his face, but instead, she asked, "So what time do you want me here in the morning?"

For some reason, Sasha Brozynski seemed determined to work for him badly enough to ignore what were obvious come-ons. Why? So she hadn't been employed for a while. Looking at her, knowing the magnitude of JoJo's ability, he had no doubt Sasha was equally talented and could have gotten another job in New York. Or anywhere. Maybe he was too suspicious, but she was JoJo's friend, after all.

Maybe she knew too much.

"Not so fast." Thinking he should find out firsthand exactly what information JoJo had passed on, he said, "You'd better see the show tonight. That way you'll have some idea of what Yale will expect from you tomorrow."

"So I'll buy a ticket."

"We're sold out." At least he hoped they were—not that she would know the difference.

"Maybe I can watch from backstage."

"I have a better idea. My private table. You'll be my guest. No arguments."

Perversely, he savored the frustration she couldn't hide. She obviously didn't want to be his guest, but she wasn't running in the other direction. Yet. And, against all logic, he didn't want to see her disappear into the night. No woman had interested him so much since Mia. That had been a lot of years, and even more women, ago.

But all women played their games and this one was no different. She wanted something from him, and he was certain the answer wasn't as simple as employment. He was also certain he would succeed in wringing it out of her, and he didn't particularly care how. He had no shame when it came to getting his way. As Vito often enjoyed reminding him, he couldn't help himself—insatiability of one kind or another was a family trait.

Attracted as hell to the stunning dancer with legs long enough to set him fantasizing, Nick wouldn't let the fact put stars in his eyes.

He'd thought a lot of JoJo, too, and look how she'd up and betrayed him....

BY THE TIME the show started, Sasha was convinced that Nick Donatelli took a perverse pleasure in making her squirm. Seated at the table smack in the middle of the Island Showroom and two levels above the stage apron that jutted out into the audience, they had the most spectacular view in the house. And snugged up next to her, Nick also had a pretty spectacular view of her legs, since her slim silk dress rode to midthigh when she sat.

He even had the audacity to place his arm around the back of her chair.

Not that he was touching her.

But he might as well be.

Nick's close proximity was disturbingly distracting. Sasha was having a difficult time paying attention to the show, the point of this assignation, after all. But rather than getting the choreography down pat—with a near-photographic memory, she was light years beyond the normal quick study—she merely registered vague impressions of the dancers' movements around the stage.

She was too aware of Nick Donatelli's body heat. Considering her main concern was her friend, and that she was trying to get this job to find JoJo, the fact ticked her off.

"Could you give me some breathing room?" she whispered, as the orchestra played a rumba and, on stage, a scantily clad woman was wooed by an ardent suitor in a sensual dance. The entire show so far had a tropical influence.

"Can't take the heat?" Nick murmured, his mouth close enough so that his breath fluttered the hair around her ear.

A shiver shot through Sasha. But she stated staunchly, "I'm a New Yorker. I can take anything you can dish out—"

"I meant the air in the room. The circulation doesn't seem to be up to par."

"Oh."

Smirking, he removed his arm and she slinked down in her seat, a bit embarrassed by the exchange. She forced herself to focus on the dancers and recognized the woman as the blonde from the dressing room.

"So what do you think?" Nick asked. "About this particular number?"

She figured he wanted her honest opinion. "The guy's fantastic. The woman's decent, but not great."

"This was JoJo's piece. Barbie was her understudy. She probably just needs some practice."

"Nope. That's not it."

"Then what is it?"

"She needs to feel the music," Sasha told him. "She's got the steps down, the body movements, too, but the music's not ingrained in her soul."

"Like it would be with you?"

"Yeah," she said, figuring she sounded nearly as arrogant as he did. "Like it would be with me." But she knew she was speaking the truth.

If she could sing as well as she danced, she might be a Broadway star by now. As things stood, she was eternally grateful that she had enough talent to ensure her steady work in an area she loved.

Sasha felt Nick's gaze on her. Intent. Unwavering. Boring into her as though he were trying to read her mind. Distracted from the dance, she glanced at him and was caught. The atmosphere grew thick with tension. Her breasts tightened and she crossed her arms to shelter herself from him. She sensed his satisfaction at her reaction.

And her wariness doubled.

Clenching her jaw, she focused her eyes on the stage, even while her mind remained behind. What kind of a game was Nick Donatelli playing with her? The attraction was real, went two ways, she had no doubt about that. But there was something else. Something he was fabricating. Or something he was concealing. She was no stranger to the darkness in people and she recognized the dangerous trait in him.

She hugged herself closer.

Somehow, she managed to direct her attention where it belonged for the next hour, on the final two-thirds of the performances. *In the Swim* was fun, a blend of sensuality and high spirits, modern dance routines and traditional show girl *prancing* as Nick had called it, surrounding performances by synchronized swimmers in a huge tank that held thousands of gallons of water. Show girls were decked out in glittery—if skimpy—costumes, the majority of plumage sprouting from the show girls' rears and heads.

Nothing *too* outrageous, thank goodness.

At the curtain call, the audience roared its approval, Sasha joining in, putting her hands together enthusiastically. When the curtain dropped, she grabbed her bag and started to rise, but Nick placed a hand over hers to stay her.

"Wait a while. No sense in getting trampled. It'll give us time to get to know one another better."

Reluctantly, she sank back into her seat as people streamed around them. "Great. Tell me about yourself."

"You know enough about me, but I know squat about you except that you and JoJo danced in a show together."

She didn't know anything about *him* other than his saving the old hotel-casino from demolition and some sketchy details about his family. "Actually, JoJo and I were roommates for a half-dozen years," she said. "And we danced together in several shows."

"So you really were good friends. Then why the separation?"

"We weren't attached at the hip. We led our own lives. She got tired of being a Broadway gypsy." JoJo might have left months earlier if Sasha hadn't needed her moral support at the time. JoJo had stayed for *her,* a loving favor Sasha was determined to return. "JoJo wanted to try something more glamorous before she was too old."

His brows lifted. "And how old are you?"

"Twenty-eight," she said without blinking an eye.

The lie was so practiced, it came naturally. In an industry where looks and age were all-important, it was a fact of life that everyone played around with one or the other or both. Tuned into that fact by the age of twenty-five, she'd chosen to count only every other birthday. If a producer knew she was thirty-two, he might not choose to hire her. She tried not to worry about what would happen a few years down the road when she couldn't fool people anymore. She didn't know anything but dancing.

"So what changed your mind? About coming west?"

"I just needed the right incentive." She was thinking about the call from JoJo, trying to remember the conversation word for word in case she'd missed any important information. But the call had been so short....

"You couldn't get work?" Nick asked.

Sasha looked him straight in the eye and truthfully said, "I didn't look for work."

And that's all she wanted to say on the matter. What had happened to her was none of his business. And if he suspected there was more to her story than her wanting a lengthy vacation, he left it alone.

She was relieved when he finally stood, saying, "I guess the rush is over."

She looked around and, indeed, the showroom was nearly empty, except for a handful of stragglers gathered near the exit doors. Nick allowed her to lead the way, though she suspected it had more to do with his enjoyment of the view than with politeness. With a spurt of defiance, she arched her back and wiggled her bottom to shake out the kinks from sitting for so long.

Once out of the theater, entering the fringe of the casino, she stopped to ask, "So what time and where should I report for my audition?"

"In the showroom at ten. I have a meeting with Yale at nine, so he'll be here."

"I won't disappoint you."

"I know you won't." He took her elbow and led her toward the opposite corner of the casino.

"Uh, where are we going now?" she asked, caution shadowing her voice.

"I wouldn't think of letting you walk to the parking lot unescorted."

"I'm a big girl—"

"So I've noticed."

And she noticed the appreciation in his gaze. Weakening, she let him have his way. Once wouldn't kill her. Although a few minutes later, when they entered a deserted hallway—obviously not a regular route to the parking lot—she was a little uptight. She didn't like dimly lit shadowy places that prompted bad memories. She was instantly on edge.

"Nervous?"

"Why would I be?"

"Thinking about auditioning gives most performers the jitters."

"I like auditioning."

She tried to concentrate on the morning, on the joy of dancing again for someone other than herself, on her hopes for finding JoJo.... But Nick wouldn't let it alone. He stopped her, crowded her against the wall, and either didn't realize she'd grown very still or was purposely ignoring the fact.

"I can make things easier for you," he murmured, his bold features drawing closer. "All you have to do is ask...."

He caught her off guard. She hadn't thought he would actually kiss her. But there his mouth was, pressed against her own. And there hers was, opening to let him in. A buzzing beset her ears and she forgot to breathe.

Automatic pilot...that's what was happening to her. Her instincts were taking over. Her attraction to a man she didn't know and probably shouldn't. Part of her wanted to push him away, part of her to draw him closer. He surrounded her, hands flat on the wall on either side of her head, but he didn't touch her. Maybe that's why she allowed the kiss. Why she returned it.

Maybe that's why the memories didn't interfere. Because he wasn't touching her.

She lost herself for a sweet, sweet moment, savoring something that had seemed lost to her—desire, hot and wet. She hadn't felt such need for any man since before last November. Six months without letting any man get too close. Six months wondering if she ever would again.

When Nick came up for air, she was breathing as hard as he. And wondering why of all men, it had to be this one that liberated her.

"I'd better get going," she murmured, starting to push past him, wanting to get away while she still could.

"Wait a minute."

When Nick unexpectedly grabbed her upper arm and pulled her around, Sasha panicked. Without thinking, she struck out, the edge of her free hand striking him hard on the neck just below his left ear. With a shout, he let go.

"What the hell is wrong with you, woman?"

What was wrong was that she wasn't about to explain why she'd done that. Even as she backed away, heart threatening to pound right out of her chest, he stood there, rubbing his neck, staring at her as if she were crazy. The fact that he wasn't coming after her even if he looked mad as hell made her realize she might have overreacted.

But what if she'd done nothing and he'd really meant to do more than detain her?

She'd be damned if she would say she was sorry.

"When a woman wants to leave," she said tersely, "let her go!"

She spun on her platform sandals and strode toward the door. She expected to hear footsteps behind her...a few curses aimed at her head, at the very least. No sound followed but the echo of her own heels. Even so, she was freaked. Painful memories surfacing, she slammed out of the hallway and raced across the parking lot, craning over her shoulder all the way to her rental car.

To think that she'd been afraid of Vito Tolentino, simply because his size had reminded her of her attacker. With his drop-dead, gorgeous looks and hot animal appeal, Nick Donatelli was the really dangerous one.

After climbing into her vehicle, she made certain the doors were locked, then sat there, shaking, her shallow breaths making her chest hurt. Frustrated and angrier with herself than she was with Nick, she slammed her hand flat against the steering wheel.

Damn, damn, damn, damn!

She couldn't let her past interfere with her present. Not to mention JoJo's future.

If her friend had one.

For the reminder of violence made Sasha face her deepest fear—that JoJo had been the latest victim and that Sasha would never see her alive again.

She couldn't think like that, Sasha warned herself. Not about JoJo. She had to concentrate on the positive. She was here now. Surely if she talked to everyone she ran into around the Caribbean, she would find *someone* who knew something that would help her track down her friend.

Chapter Three

"C'mon, Nick, say you'll have dinner with us tonight." Pacing the length of his penthouse office, Caroline Donatelli was trying her very best to coax her stubborn brother into agreeing. "Papa says it's been so long since he's seen you that he's forgotten what you look like."

Desk chair turned half away from her so that he was staring out the window, Nick rubbed the left side of his neck as if it were bothering him. "So show him my picture."

Her brother was distracted in a way that told Caroline only a woman could be responsible. She sighed. Another one, and so soon. She was getting tired of cleaning up his messes. Would he never learn?

She stopped her pacing and leaned against the window in front of him, fingers worrying the folds of her dress, the fine silk the same bright green that matched her and Nick's eyes. "Don't take that attitude, please. Papa loves you."

Nick ran his hand through the thick dark hair that was the inheritance of all three Donatelli siblings. "And I love him," he said gruffly. "I didn't mean anything by that. I'm just real busy lately."

Right. Busy getting himself involved with another woman unworthy of him. Caroline clenched inside. She'd felt this way several times when he'd gotten involved with his troublesome paramours—starting with Mia Scudella, the haughty little chit who had tried to pry him away from the family nearly a dozen years before.

Now who was he hung up on?

Caroline kept her anger in check, but allowed the right amount of hurt to color her tone when she asked, "Are you really too busy for your own family? You've been ignoring us ... purposely ... and you know it."

He turned an eerie gaze on her. "I've had a lot on my mind."

When he looked at her like that, the green eyes so like her own, searing her, trying to see through her, Caroline feared *he knew.* Is that why he'd stopped coming around *Donatelli's?* He used to have dinner with her and Papa a lot, usually once a week, but it had been nearly two months since he'd shown his face at the family's restaurant, which boasted the best Italian food in Las Vegas.

Was he avoiding *her?*

The thought that he might be personally rejecting her made Caroline sick inside. It was bad enough that Nick refused to work in the family business, that he'd struck out on his own. So he'd saved one little outdated elephant of a hotel-casino from the grave. Big deal. He could be building an empire more extensive than her father had ever controlled.

Rather, they could be building it together.

For Caroline had never hidden her ambitious streak—and Papa would never turn the business over to her control alone. She was only a woman, after all, and in Salvatore Donatelli's eyes that meant she should be barefoot and pregnant, not in charge of a multimillion-dollar corporation.

If only Lucky hadn't hightailed it out of Las Vegas years ago, she would have options. But she couldn't even remember the last time she'd heard from the younger brother who'd once said the Donatelli siblings were the *Three Musketeers* and someday would take the world by storm together.

That left Nick to take over—with her at his side, of course—or Papa would put some outsider in charge.

Caroline couldn't tolerate the idea. She was a Donatelli, had the Donatelli pride, no matter her sex.

She stepped closer, placing a hand on the shoulder of the older brother she'd idolized since they were kids. She couldn't stop herself from testing him. Her stomach lurched. She had to know that he still cared.

She pleaded with him, "Please, Nick, come to dinner for *me.*" She held her breath, fearing he would reject her.

But then he finally agreed. "All right, but I can't tonight. Maybe tomorrow."

The half promise allowed her to breathe again. "Tomorrow for sure," she said. "Okay?"

"I'll try." Checking his watch, he rose from the chair, once more seeming distracted. "Right now I have some business to attend to."

Business that involved the new woman?

"I understand," Caroline said, walking with him to the front door. "I'll be looking forward to seeing you tomorrow night, then. I'll tell Papa you'll be there."

And in the meantime, Caroline thought as they headed for the elevator, she'd hang around to see if she couldn't get a glimpse of Nick's newest distraction.

FIGURING SHOWING UP to audition was an exercise in futility—certain that Nick Donatelli wouldn't want her to darken his doorstep again after she'd hauled off and whomped him the night before—Sasha entered the Island Showroom on time anyway, JoJo's welfare uppermost on her mind. If this Yale Riker were around, perhaps she could bold it out. No one had ever accused her of not having guts.

To her surprise, a slim man wearing loose purple pants and a sleeveless lilac T-shirt had center stage. Keeping time in his head, he was running through a series of dance steps she recognized from the night before. The rumba. Only he wasn't dancing the man's part, but the blonde's.

Smothering a grin, thinking he was doing a smashing job, Sasha moved through the darkened theater until she was standing mere yards from the stage. In the middle of a turn, the man spotted her and came to an abrupt halt.

"You must be Sasha Brozynski," he said with enthusiasm. "Love the name, darling. It's so...ethnic."

Sasha laughed. "I'm third generation. My dad's parents were from Poland, my mom's from Ukraine."

"A regular eastern European melting pot. I'm Yale Riker." He held out his hand. "Come on up here so I can get a better view of the whole package."

He was stronger than he looked. Though Sasha was definitely taller and probably weighed more, he gave her the boost she needed to hop onto the stage without going around to the stairs. His slim body was solid with the musculature of a dancer, so he obviously kept up with his first love, even though he was now a choreographer and producer. He was a nice-looking man with finely cut features, his deep tan accentuated by light brown hair, artfully streaked blond.

Yale circled Sasha, making little "Mmm" and "Ah-hah" sounds as he inspected her as carefully as Nick had. This time, however, she had no sense of sexual interest in the study, and definitely would have been surprised if she had.

Amused by the thought, she asked, "Will I do?"

"Do? You're stunning, darling. Look at those marvelous legs. Those marvelous breasts. That marvelous mane of hair." After enumerating her attributes, making her feel a bit like a prized racehorse, he gave her a mournful expression. "Now please, please tell me you really can dance as fabulously as you claimed to Mr. D."

Amazed and pleased that Nick hadn't held her overblown reaction of the night before against her, she laughed again. "I really can."

He brightened. "Good. Then let's begin. Put your bag over there. I'll show you a few steps from one of our numbers, then I'll turn on the music and see what you can do with them on your own."

Sasha did as he asked. She was prepared, already wearing rehearsal clothes—hot-pink-and-orange shorts over hot-pink tights and a hot-pink leotard with a cut-out midriff, and medium heeled shoes with buckled straps over the insteps.

The routine he demonstrated was the same as he'd been practicing when she'd walked in on him—the rumba. She shouldn't be surprised. She'd given Nick her honest opinion of the blonde's performance and had agreed that she could do better. Through Yale, he was challenging her to do so.

Before she began, she gave the audience a quick once-over to make certain he wasn't sitting there spying on her. Though she had great vision, she couldn't cut through the dark. She didn't feel Nick Donatelli's presence, anyway, and she suspected she would if he were there.

"Ready to try it?" Yale asked when he'd run through the short segment twice. "Or do you want me to go over everything again?"

"If I forget something, I'll improvise," she promised.

"Good enough."

Holding out his hand to indicate she should wait a moment, he turned on the tape player and, finding the right spot, gave her the signal.

Already swaying to the rhythm, absorbing the music, running the choreography through her mind, Sasha began. She concentrated on her opening steps, made them smooth and sure. And then she was on automatic, doing what, for her, came naturally. As she lost herself to the seductive rhythm of the dance, her imagination started working overtime and she conjured up an illusory partner.

Nick Donatelli.

Remembering how he'd gotten under her skin the night before, she used it. She danced for him alone, her body a slave to the sensual music. She envisioned his own long limbs joining her. Close. So close. In her head, they moved together as one. Sinuous. Throbbing with repressed passion. She could almost feel his breath on her face, his hands on her hips, long fingers spread, cupping her to him...

Until the heady music abruptly ended.

Taken aback, Sasha faltered and snapped back to reality. Had her dicey hormones just lost her this job? She faced Yale Riker, steeling herself against disappointment.

But he was throwing back his head, yelling, "Yes! There is a God!"

Relieved, Sasha grinned.

And from the audience came the sound of clapping.

Her grin faded. She knew the solitary source before she saw him. No imagination this time. Her pulse raced crazily. He was coming down the aisle—stride long and deliberate, hard gaze on her, features expressionless.

Nick Donatelli in the flesh.

NICK COULDN'T BELIEVE Sasha Brozynski could turn him on again after the cold shower she'd given him the night before. But lost to the rhythm of that dance, she had. Just as she would turn on every man who came to see the show. The businessman in him was ecstatic at such a find. The rest of him was none too thrilled, and he was further unthrilled speculating as to why that might be.

"Mr. D, you're a genius!" Yale raved. "She's exactly what we need."

Sasha Brozynski wasn't what he needed. She was trouble. He'd known that when he'd pushed her with his come-ons. He'd definitely known that when he'd kissed her. What puzzled him was her reaction when he'd tried to stop her from leaving. For a moment, she'd lost it. As she'd lashed out, fear had shone from her eyes.

Of him?

He could hardly blame her.

If she were smart, she'd stay the hell away from him. If she were brilliant, she'd turn tail and run back to New

York City, familiar territory where she could tell the bad guys from the good. Things here were more complicated.

"You weren't exaggerating about your talent," Nick admitted.

"Thank you."

"I'll work her into the show immediately," Yale was saying, speaking as much to himself as to either of them. He paced the stage, ticking off his plans aloud. "First, the rumba. Definitely, the rumba. Barbie will have a hissy fit, but the poor dear just doesn't have what it takes to rise above the chorus line. Next, we'll work on the opening and closing numbers, of course. I'm certain we can be ready in a day or two..."

"Then I have the job?"

Nick moved closer until he could see the sheen of perspiration making Sasha's skin glow. He followed a trickle that disappeared into her cleavage and imagined what it would be like putting that sheen on her personally. His groin tightened and he was hard-pressed to hide the fact.

"It's yours," he said, thinking she took the pronouncement awful calmly for a dancer who'd been out of work for six months—another puzzle—when all she did was say, "Great."

Yale didn't seem to notice. He went on with his typical savoir faire. "I'll finish taking you over the choreography for the rumba before lunch. I just can't wait to see the wonder you create with the rest of the number! We'll have all afternoon to rehearse. Ah, nirvana!" Suddenly he started and focused on her. "You don't have other plans?"

"No. I'm all yours."

Sasha addressed Yale, but she was looking straight at him, Nick realized. "I'll expect you to sit in on both shows with me tonight—once from backstage so you can get a feel for the flow of the big numbers." And so he could get a better feel for her. "We're dark tomorrow night."

"Even if there's no show tomorrow, we can rehearse," Yale added. "I'll have to think of something to bribe your rumba partner to give up his day off. And I'll have the entire cast arrive early on Wednesday to run through the open and close!"

Figuring Yale had the situation under control, wondering why the hell he'd gone and committed himself to spending the evening with the woman who'd turned on him as fast as she'd turned him on, Nick backed off. Sasha's focus was already on the choreographer, who immediately began work.

A sudden noise from the back of the showroom whipped Nick around to scan the darkened house. Someone was up there, silently watching. The sound of a phone ringing made him glance back at the stage to see Yale answering a call on his cellular. He returned his interest to the house in time to catch a sliver of light as an entrance door closed.

He rushed up the steps, determined to see who had been spying on him.

A moment later, flying through the doorway, he nearly tripped over floor-cleaning equipment parked a yard or so away. Shins stinging, Nick cursed.

"Mr. D, you all right?" asked Lester Perkins, punching at the glasses that sat crooked on his nose. The mousy maintenance man seemed upset. "You're not hurt or nothing, are you?"

Nick ignored the fussing. "Were you inside the theater just now?"

"Not yet. I was getting my stuff together. Is there a problem?"

"No. No problem."

If not Lester, then who? Frowning, Nick moved off toward the casino in time to see a familiar green skirt disappear into the crowd.

Caroline.

What the hell was his sister up to this time?

SASHA WAS DISAPPOINTED that she didn't get anything out of Yale about JoJo, except praise for her friend's talent as a dancer. She'd subtly questioned him, just as she intended to do with everyone she came in contact with at the Caribbean. But if no one knew anything...

As she rummaged through her bag for a comb, a man cleared his throat. "Those were some great moves."

She jumped and looked down into a pair of hazel eyes magnified by thick glasses. "Thanks," she told the maintenance man, who'd been efficiently, if silently, mopping floors for the past hour. His bony frame was covered by a turquoise coverall that had somehow remained clean, and his brown hair was neatly combed away from a face so homely that even a mother would have trouble finding something to admire in it.

"Best I seen around here lately," he added, ducking his head shyly.

Finding her comb, she ran it through her tangled hair. "Have you worked here long?"

"Since the place reopened." He was mopping the floor as he spoke. "Used to work for Mr. D's father for nearly twenty years before that. Name's Lester Perkins."

"Hi. Sasha Brozynski." She gauged the man to be no more than forty. That meant he'd been working for a Donatelli for his entire adult life . . . even though the elder Donatelli had been in prison much of that time. "So, I guess you like working for Mr. D—uh, Donatelli?"

"You bet. Great boss." His expression grew wistful. "And he's some kinda man, ain't he?"

Swiping a coat of protective gloss over her lips, she agreed, "Some kind."

The kind she should avoid like the plague. She dropped the gloss into her shoulder bag. So why had she imagined dancing for him . . . with him?

She'd be dancing with danger.

"You're new," Lester said.

"Fresh from New York." Thinking she'd better go if she was going to get some lunch herself, she shouldered her bag and hopped down to the floor.

But before she could take her leave, Lester said, "JoJo's from New York."

That stopped her cold. "You know JoJo?"

"My favorite show girl. She's real nice to me. Talks to me sometimes."

Wondering if Lester might have some clue as to what happened to her friend, Sasha leaned back against the stage and asked, "What did you talk about?"

"Lots of things."

"Her boyfriends?"

His expression clouded over. "She shouldn't of thrown over Mr. D. That wasn't nice."

"Mr. D?" That one knocked her for a loop. "JoJo was going out with Nick Donatelli?"

"Until a coupla weeks ago."

A couple of weeks? And then JoJo had met, fallen in love with and been planning on marrying someone else? "So who is she going out with now?"

Lester shrugged and went back to his mopping.

But, her hope refueled, Sasha refused to give up so easily. "JoJo went off without leaving me word. You wouldn't know where, would you?"

He didn't even look her way when he stridently told her, "I said she talked to me. Didn't say she discussed her secrets with me!"

Secrets. What kind of secrets? Sasha's heart skipped a beat. The supposed marriage seemed to be one. Maybe Lester Perkins *did* know something.

"It's just that I'm really worried about JoJo," she told him anxiously. "I came here because she asked me to. If you think of anything she might have said . . ."

"Uh-huh."

When Lester didn't even slow a mop stroke, Sasha knew she was being dismissed. Frustration renewed, she swept out of the showroom, aimlessly crossing the casino, her mind moving faster than her feet.

JoJo and Nick Donatelli. She couldn't feature it. Weird. She and JoJo had never gone gaga over the same man—not ever—and she couldn't deny her own attraction to the owner of the Caribbean. Now she felt funny about it, as if she were betraying the Girlfriends' Code or something. Rule 1: Never compete for the same guy. Then again, according to Lester, JoJo had dumped Nick. Besides, JoJo had planned on marrying someone else, for heaven's sake. Right?

Hadn't she?

Not having known about JoJo and Nick before, Sasha hadn't done any speculating in that direction. But now the possibility hit her smack between the eyes.

What if Nick was *the Hunkman* that JoJo had been planning to marry...? And then what if Nick had changed his mind and JoJo had tried to hold him to the agreement...?

Skin crawling, Sasha wasn't certain she wanted to take that leap forward.

The first thing she had to do was to see what she could find out about Nick and JoJo's relationship. How long? How far? How intense? But how, how, how was she supposed to do that?

Searching every inch of her friend's apartment would be a good start. She'd been in such a tizzy the day before, she hadn't even thought about doing so.

Blinking back to reality, Sasha realized she was on the Strip and heading south, far enough from her car that she could just about walk to JoJo's place in the same amount of time it would take her to hotfoot it back to the lot. Sasha rushed down the street, head held high, despite the rash of tourists who were staring at her gaudy pink-and-orange rehearsal gear, which had to look pretty odd on the street, even for Vegas.

"Hey, you looking for a date, sugar?" drawled a middle-aged man, who wore shorts that settled below his paunch and a too-tight knit shirt that accentuated it.

"If I were, I wouldn't be looking here," she sing-songed, so used to getting more direct propositions on the streets of Manhattan, this one didn't even make her break stride.

Still, not wanting to be bothered when she had so much on her mind, she decided to get off the Strip and take a back street. The opportunity came with a construction site for the Wild West, a hotel-casino that was being expanded. The new tower of additional rooms and suites was already up, as was the skeleton of a new multistory garage. But machinery was still humming . . . and construction workers were still whistling. At her.

She waved to the leering hard hats as she sailed by the chain-link fencing. "Don't let those eyes bug out too far, boys," she yelled good-naturedly, "or you might fall and get hurt!"

Wolf whistles followed her out the corridor and onto the semiresidential street that ran parallel with the Strip. But Sasha's mind was already floating in another world. Nick and JoJo. Was it really possible?

And if Nick had had something going with her friend, why had he been hitting on *her?*

The last question especially bothered Sasha, probably because her attraction to Nick was more important to her than she'd been willing to admit. He'd brought her womanliness alive when she'd thought it might be permanently out of commission. And, truthfully, no man had ever gotten to her the way he had. Not ever.

The men she was used to dating treated her differently, more on an equal footing or even deferentially, perhaps because she could be a little intimidating. The strength of her personality—if he even recognized it— seemed to mean squat to Nick Donatelli. He was such a forceful male presence that he made her feel more . . . what?

Certainly not helpless. She'd proven she could take care of herself, even with Nick.

Feminine? Maybe that was it. As tall and imposing as she had been from the age of eleven on, she'd always had difficulty feeling something that should come naturally to any woman.

She put that speculation behind her as she approached JoJo's apartment building and mentally prepared herself for the search. Maybe now she would recognize some truths that had been staring her in the face all along.

Sasha started in the living area, checking drawers and shelves. She found JoJo's old scrapbook and hoped that it would hold a key to her romantic life. She quickly flipped through all the old photos and theater programs, recognizing many, getting misty-eyed at the shots of the two of them that her friend obviously still treasured.

To her disappointment, the chronicle of JoJo's professional and personal life stopped shortly after she'd arrived in Las Vegas—a few photos of the glitzy hotels, a program from her current show and several shots of JoJo with performers and other employees of the Caribbean. One picture did catch her eye, however—the dealer she'd seen in Nick's penthouse was standing with JoJo and the blonde named Barbie. Barbie had categorically denied knowing anything about JoJo's current romantic life, yet, in this photograph, they seemed pretty chummy, arms wrapped around each other's waists.

Finding nothing more revealing, Sasha replaced the scrapbook on its shelf and continued looking. When she'd exhausted all the drawers and nooks and crannies of the living area and kitchen, she started on the bedroom.

The nightstand held JoJo's birth control but no clue as to the man she had been using it with. Likewise, the chest of drawers and closet held nothing that sparked Sasha's interest, not even when she climbed on a chair to inspect the higher shelves more closely.

All that was left was the mirrored dresser and the jewelry box on top.

Knowing what she would find inside, Sasha opened the box. A sparkly pin reminded her of the last show she and JoJo had danced in together. And there was the bracelet from the one before. And the earrings her friend had bought to celebrate the job previous to that. She suspected the pearl choker with the jet front clasp was her Las Vegas addition. Superstitious, as were many performers, JoJo always bought herself an expensive piece of costume jewelry on opening night for luck. About to close the box, Sasha spotted something odd amongst the contents. She pulled out a key attached to a rhinestone-studded ring—a gambling chip with the Caribbean scrawled across it.

Full-size, this was no safe-deposit box or locker key, but a key to a door's dead bolt. She knew it wouldn't open the front door, but she headed for the kitchen to try it on the back. Not a fit. Something stopped Sasha from returning the key to the jewelry box.

Something told her this might be her key to the intended groom, that it might fit his place. Now if she could only find the right door...one *at* the Caribbean?

After slipping the key into her shoulder bag, she continued her search through the dresser. Nothing but clothes. Then she opened the last drawer. Riffling through JoJo's nightwear—far sexier than any Sasha remembered her wearing when they were roommates—she felt something skitter to the back. She went after what turned out to be an eight-by-ten envelope. A package some unknown person had given to JoJo. Only her name was printed in plain block letters.

What in the world was this doing in with JoJo's nightclothes?

Sasha sat back on the floor, the envelope practically burning her fingers. Her pulse picked up. Instinct told her JoJo had put the envelope in that drawer not by mistake but to hide it.

Something of importance had to be inside.

Taking a deep, calming breath, Sasha shook the contents from the envelope. Copies of newspaper clippings floated down to the rug. After reading the headlines, checking the photos and scanning the accompanying stories, she leaned back against the bed in shock.

Some of the articles were about a murder that had taken place nearly a dozen years before. A young woman, Mia Scudella, daughter of a crime family, had been found slain behind the family business, a knife through her heart.

The rest of the stories, dated a few months ago—just before JoJo had arrived in town—were about a show girl named Glory Hale, whose body had been found at the very construction site Sasha had passed on the way here. The show girl, too, had been stabbed through the heart.

One other thing connected the victims—the thing that made her sick inside. Both women had been linked to the same man, one who had been suspect but never arrested. Both women had thrown him over shortly before their deaths.

Nick Donatelli!

Drop-dead gorgeous just took on a whole new meaning for her.

Chapter Four

"Everyone, gather, gather, gather!" Yale Riker ordered the Caribbean's company of dancers between shows. "I want you to meet our newest—" he sighed dramatically "—show girl."

Barbie stared through slitted eyes at the tawny-maned woman who'd come looking for JoJo Weston the day before. She'd said she was interested in work. Obviously Nick Donatelli had been interested in her.

And Barbie didn't like it, not one bit. She'd never liked serious competition, in either her professional or her personal life. Smiling through gritted teeth, however, she was the first to extend a hand full of fake, two-inch, hot-pink nails.

"Welcome to *In the Swim*," she said, referring to the Island Showroom's current production. "I'm Barbie Doll. Stage name," she hurriedly added over the snickers behind her.

Recognition and something else—guilt?—flickered through the amber eyes of the Amazon, as Barbie chose to think of the other woman.

"Sasha Brozynski. Sasha's short for Alexandra, and the last name is for real."

While other dancers chuckled at the good-humored return, Barbie merely maintained her forced smile and faded into the woodwork as introductions were made all around. She wanted to size up her new rival.

Unfortunately, Barbie didn't like what she saw any more than she had the day before. The longest pair of legs in the chorus line. The lushest—and possibly real— hair. And the most natural smile, with blindingly white teeth.

The Amazon could represent a toothpaste company, for crying out loud!

"You'll all be coming in an hour early on Wednesday," Yale was saying. "Sasha's a fast learner and we're going to rehearse a few numbers again tomorrow. She'll be in the opener and closer for starters, and we'll need to run through those with her several times before the first show."

A few of the dancers groaned, but no one protested. No one argued with Yale Riker unless they were nuts. While he normally swished around the stage and enthused all over everyone, Barbie thought, the little fairy had a will of steel and a temper of fire when that will was thwarted.

And it couldn't be more obvious that he was enamored of the Amazon.

Barbie wanted to scream. Having put up with JoJo for months had been bad enough. They'd been rivals for a couple of leads and a duo, each having won out at one time or another. If this one danced as good as Barbie feared she might, she had the potential to steal the whole damned show.

And now, feeling that she was at last—and deservedly so—on top, Barbie wasn't about to let that happen. Not after finally having gotten rid of JoJo.

So when Yale indicated that Sasha was going to hang around backstage during the late show to see how things operate, Barbie volunteered, "And in the meantime, I can give her the two-bit tour and warn her about our demanding choreographer and producer."

Rather than smiling as he was supposed to, Yale had that strange look in his eyes. "Let's chat, first," he suggested, dismissing the others with a brush of his hand. Then he looked at the Amazon and pointed to the props area. "Sasha, could you wait over there for Barbie?"

"Sure."

Sasha ambled away and Barbie gave Yale her sweetest smile. "What's up?"

"I might as well put it to you straight, darling," he said with a sigh. "Starting Wednesday night, Sasha will be dancing the rumba with Lance."

Unprepared for this blow, Barbie started, open-mouthed. "You've got to be kidding."

"Afraid not."

"But you just gave *me* the number. What's going on here? Did Mr. D get into her panties already?"

"That's enough," Yale said, the steel suddenly making an appearance. "No need to be crude. Partnering her with Lance was *my* decision, though Mr. D did agree."

And Barbie knew well enough Yale didn't fancy getting into any female's panties . . . unless maybe to wear them once in a while.

"Can I ask why?"

"A strictly professional decision. The rumba seems to be her dance."

A nice, if cowardly, way of saying that Sasha had more talent than she did. While Yale droned on—now praising her own abilities and assuring her that no one would think any the less of her—Barbie shut him out and searched for the Amazon, who was studying the floor in front of her feet.

The bitch knew!

Hot jealousy seared Barbie, and she vowed to make her newest rival pay.

SASHA COULD TELL that Barbie hadn't taken the news well—who would?—but the blonde was putting up a good front, all smiles and compliments, and ignoring what had to be eating at her. Sasha figured it was up to her to broach the topic if she wanted the other woman's cooperation.

"Barbie, I'm sorry about Yale assigning me your number."

Her gray eyes going flat, the other dancer said, "Don't. Why should you be?"

"Because I don't like hurting people."

"Really. Then why didn't you say no?"

"It was professional, not personal. I mean, I needed the job." Had to have it if she was ever going to figure out what happened to JoJo. How else could she get close to the people who knew her friend? "How would it have looked if I'd said no to Yale?"

Barbie's expression changed subtly. "You're right, of course. It's just that I loved that piece so. I put everything I had into it."

Sasha let it drop. She wasn't going to lie and say she could tell from the way Barbie danced it. Maybe that had been her all, though. Probably was. Some dancers were just more blessed than others. Waiting until after she'd had the grand tour of the facilities—dressing rooms, props, technical booth—Sasha then broached the topic that was nearly consuming her.

"Say, you haven't heard from JoJo, have you?" she asked as they left the room from which audio and lighting, backdrops and the human fish tank were controlled.

"No. You?"

Sasha sighed. "I wish."

"I wouldn't worry about her. She's probably off on some romantic honeymoon."

"Yeah, no doubt you're right," Sasha lied. Even if she had done something so impulsive, JoJo would have gotten word to her by now. Something untoward had definitely happened. "But who was this guy? Didn't you have any clue that she was nuts about someone?"

She was hoping that, though Barbie had pleaded ignorance earlier, the blonde knew something she hadn't shared.

"Lately? Nope."

"What about not so lately?"

Sasha held her breath until Barbie confirmed it. "Nick Donatelli."

"Really?" she said, as if the maintenance man hadn't already told her.

"Really."

"When was that?"

"JoJo broke off with him a couple of weeks ago."

Thinking about the packet of articles she'd found, Sasha asked, "You wouldn't know why, would you?" as they strolled through the theater and toward the stage.

"We weren't exactly confidantes."

"How about an educated guess."

Barbie grew thoughtful. "She probably couldn't put up with Mr. D."

"What do you mean?" Thinking the other woman knew something after all, Sasha pressed her nails into her palms. "Is he abusive to women?"

"He's definitely a lady-killer, but I haven't seen any bruises on anyone."

"What do you mean by *anyone?*"

"The show girls." Leading the way up the side steps to the stage, Barbie stopped and turned, gazing straight into her eyes. "Mr. D goes through them like salted peanuts—he isn't satisfied with just one."

Put off by the distasteful comparison, Sasha asked, "Are you sure the split between him and JoJo was permanent?"

"It's pretty obvious, isn't it? JoJo's gone and Mr. D's still here."

Before turning to lead the way backstage, Barbie's expression turned devious, confusing Sasha. Did the blonde really believe JoJo and Nick had been quits, or did she suspect her employer of foul play?

After finding the copies of the newspaper articles, all kinds of horrible speculations had plagued Sasha. Worst case, JoJo had been stabbed through the heart like the other two women, only her body hadn't yet been found. Of course, that was taking a big leap. First, while Nick had been connected to the crimes because of his relationship with both women, he had never been arrested. And, second, she had no real reason to suspect that JoJo had been murdered in the same way.

Or murdered at all, for that matter.

Sasha only prayed that everyone was correct in thinking her friend had eloped . . . though, if that were the case, she herself might strangle JoJo when she saw her next.

"You've got yourself all tied up in knots, don't you?" Barbie commented sympathetically. "Relax, already. You're in the Southwest, now. We don't run on Eastern time. Things are a little more relaxed out here than in New York City. I'm certain there's nothing to worry about and that JoJo will pop out of the woodwork when you least expect her to show."

But Barbie's gray eyes were cold, making Sasha start. She remembered the blonde's reaction to *her* the day before. Resentment? Jealousy? Then, again, considering the circumstances, who could blame her? At least Barbie was trying to put on a good face, which was more than many performers would do in her situation.

"I certainly hope you're right."

"Oh, well, I'd better pamper my tootsies while I can—get comfortable in the dressing room and put them up. Next show starts in little more than half an hour."

Sasha took a quick gander through the opening in the curtain now behind her. Indeed, the showroom doors had already opened and audience members were being seated efficiently, and waitresses draped in flower prints reminiscent of the islands were already taking their drink orders.

"Thanks for the tour."

Barbie waved and hurried off.

Not knowing where to go from there—while Nick had sat through the early show with her yet again, who knew where he'd disappeared to—Sasha kept busy staying out of everyone's way for the next few minutes.

The stagehands were setting up for the opening number that involved the water tank. An acrobatic team—composed of Olympic-class gymnasts from an eastern European country—was warming up backstage. And suddenly the technical director came rushing through, issuing instructions to his crew through a portable headset.

Finally, Sasha found a safe spot in a corner where she could see without being trampled.

And where she could think without being interrupted. Could mull over the bits and pieces she'd been gathering about Nick Donatelli.

She'd taken the time to read the articles someone had sent JoJo about the murders. Had that particular "surprise package" been the reason she'd broken off with Nick?

According to the tabloids, Nick Donatelli was every inch the lady-killer Barbie had professed him to be.

But was he really, in the true sense of the word?

While she'd gotten a gander at Nick with at least a half-dozen different women hanging on his arm in the photos accompanying the clippings, that didn't make him a murderer. Yes, he'd been suspect, questioned by the police after each of the two deaths.

Nearly a dozen years before, Mia Scudella had been officially engaged to Nick for several months before she'd suddenly broken off the relationship. No explanation as to why. When she'd been found slain a couple weeks later, Nick had been picked up for questioning, but he'd never been arrested because of his alibi.

Vito Tolentino, the man who'd put Sasha on red alert both times she'd had contact with him, had vouched for Nick's whereabouts at the time of the murder. Because of the breakup, they'd been getting drunk together at his place, Vito had maintained, and Nick had never been out of his sight.

Further reading had made her aware that Vito was very much Salvatore Donatelli's man. For many years he'd been bodyguard not only to Sally's heir apparent, Nick, but also to his younger children, Caroline and Lucian. Vito's loyalty went unquestioned.

Except by the justice system, she thought wryly.

For the killer had never been caught, and Mia Scudella's murder remained unsolved to this day.

And Vito Tolentino had provided a second alibi for the man he now shadowed.

The night show girl Glory Hale died on the Wild West construction site—this time within days of breaking off her relationship with Nick—Vito had claimed he and Nick were conferring about some high rollers who were staying at the hotel. He'd maintained they'd been discussing perks and incentives for the group, and that they'd made some plans for a private game. According to Vito, this one-on-one conference had lasted well into the night, after which he had cooked them both an omelet, which they'd finished as the sun crept over the horizon—hours after Glory's murder.

Vito was obviously a man of many talents.

But was one of those talents lying convincingly?

Had Vito covered for Nick as Sally Donatelli expected him to, or had he been telling the truth? The authorities had accepted his word, even as the newspapers continued speculating. Now she was speculating. Fearing for her friend's life.

What if Nick Donatelli were a murderer?

How would she ever know?

An idea crept into her conscious against her will. The words "crazy," "ridiculous," and definitely "unsmart" came to mind. She was no cop. She wasn't trained, for God's sake, except for one lousy course in self-defense. But who else could do it? Who else would?

She'd tried contacting the authorities about JoJo's disappearance, and they'd basically kissed her off with the forty-eight-hour routine. So she'd gotten a job as a show girl for the Caribbean, figuring that would do the trick.

Well, just talking to people to get to the truth wouldn't. Now she knew she had to get closer to Nick Donatelli himself. Knew she would have to dance with danger to learn the truth.

Her mouth went dry at the prospect of making Nick Donatelli fall head over heels for her. As she plotted, her palms began to sweat, betraying her nerves. A pulsing in her belly belied her excitement. She didn't want to think too hard about exactly what would be expected of her to achieve this goal. And then, when he was properly enthralled, Sasha knew she would have to give him the big kiss-off.

And if Nick were the murderer, he'd come for her as he had for the others....

A sudden squeeze of her upper arm nearly sent her skyrocketing off the floor. "What the—!"

"Whoa," Nick said, ducking away from her as if fearing she would slug him again. "I told you I'd be back."

Heart pounding furiously, Sasha put on a tremulous smile and murmured, "So...welcome back...Nicky."

NICKY?

Nick hated the endearment, hadn't allowed anyone to call him that since his mother died. He scowled at Sasha, but she gave him a wide-eyed look that threw him. Chemistry was not a question. Her accepting it and actually flirting with him was. A definite reversal of attitude.

Why?

Another game?

Two could play this game, Nick thought, moving in on her. His eyes dropped from her seductive little smile to linger at the expanse of skin revealed from her throat to the swells of her breasts. Nothing to complain about, that was for certain. She was wearing a short, tight red number under a bolero jacket trimmed with a black silk design that appeared Oriental in origin. He was a man who noticed what women wore. And appreciated. He was appreciating the hell out of her outfit at the moment.

"Miss me?" he asked.

"Mmm."

His eyebrows slashed upward. "How much?"

"Enough."

Ready for any of her sudden movements—his neck was still sore for crissakes—he slid a hand around her waist until he could pull her a bit closer. "Good. Then you'll like my plans for the rest of the night."

"What plans?"

Nick figured she wanted his hand right where it sat— the tips of his fingers on the swell of her buttocks—or she would remove it. Or remove herself. And yet, something in her expression put him on guard, like maybe this was part of the game, one he was determined to figure out.

"After the show," he said, "I thought we'd stop in on a private poker game."

Actually, he'd meant to do so all along, as usual, but he'd only thought of taking her along just now.

"I don't gamble," she said, a funny little catch in her breath.

"Neither do I." Not with money. Definitely not with women. Not anymore. He would make certain the odds were stacked in his favor. "I arranged the game for some high rollers who are staying here at the hotel. They should be entering the presidential suite even as we speak."

Interest sparked her amber eyes. "Where would that be?"

"Top floor."

"Really. Then it's right near your apartment?"

"Down the hall from my place."

Testing, ready to duck if necessary, he inched her even closer so that her lush body was millimeters from his own. She didn't fight it but went with the flow.

"Nicky, isn't this a bit public...?"

Her coy attitude not lost on him, he glanced around. "I don't know about that," he said, unable to help himself from torturing her a bit. "We're out of the mainstream of traffic. No one's paying us the least bit of mind. And if they did, so what?"

Torture. That's what he was doing to *himself*, getting her this close and not being able to act on the tightening in his groin. Even he wouldn't be crude enough to take a woman where prying eyes could see...no matter how much the fantasy appealed to him.

"I wouldn't want people to think I got this job just because I...well, you know."

"Because you might be sleeping with the boss? Angel, that wouldn't turn a head around here."

He very carefully gauged her reaction. Women wanted him. He wasn't naive. Some wanted more—the luxury that came with the territory. But he'd swear she wasn't after anything that had to do with money. And, while that chemistry was real—her face was flushed, and not just with embarrassment—he sensed she was forcing herself to accept it.

He didn't know why, but he let her off the hook for the moment—let go when he wanted to explore her far more intimately. Her lashes fluttered, and a sigh that was undoubtedly one of relief whispered through her full lips—lips that were painted a deep red and that reminded him of ripe fruit.

Every bit of Sasha Brozynski was luscious and ripe for the picking. And he would do so, Nick vowed. In his own time. No matter her game. Recognizing that she was playing pliant because she wanted something of him, he had the advantage. And he was always one to take his advantages where he could.

Chapter Five

Having been handed an unexpected advantage on a silver platter, Sasha determined to make the most of the opportunity. A high-roller game on the same floor as Nick's penthouse—*what luck!* Maybe she would be willing to gamble a bit, after all.

As they crossed through the showroom, empty but for the waitresses clearing the drink glasses and collecting their tips, Nick's hand pressed into the small of her back. The warmth he created in her made Sasha squirm. And feel a little guilty about her plans, the most immediate of which was to find a way to try the key she'd secreted in her shoulder bag on Nick's penthouse door. Undoubtedly it would do little more than confirm what she already knew—that he and JoJo had been lovers.

Unless, of course, she had time to get inside and take a thorough look around....

"So how do you feel about getting on stage in just two days?" Nick asked as they stepped out of the theater and into the boundaries of the casino.

"Great."

"No reservations?"

Distracted by the noise, Sasha lost her focus for a moment. Long enough to notice a dark-haired woman sitting at a nearby slot machine, her attention not on the one-armed bandit, but focused on them. What was the interest? Sasha gave her a curious look in return, and the woman in green silk immediately turned away, busying herself with her purse as if she might be searching for change to play the slots.

Sasha shrugged off the incident, crediting her imagination with fabrication.

Realizing that Nick was expecting a reply, she leaned into him and said, "I'm a quick study, Nicky. And Yale seems to think I'm doing all right."

"He thinks better of you than that... but that's not what I'm getting at."

"What, then?"

"I was wondering why someone with your talent hasn't worked in so long."

A subject she wanted to avoid. "I needed a rest."

"Odd that you would take an extended vacation while a show was still playing rather than after it closed."

"It wasn't exactly a planned vacation. I had an... accident." She had, in a manner of speaking. "I needed some time to recuperate. My spot in the chorus line was filled."

And fear had kept her from looking for another one. At least another in New York City.

"What kind of accident?" Nick asked. "Car?"

"That's a little personal, don't you think?"

He slid his hand on an angle to cup one hip. "I thought we were getting personal."

Sasha clenched her jaw. He had her there. To further her plan, she'd played up to him throughout the entire second show. He'd stolen another kiss from her when she hadn't been alert enough to duck the pass.

Her intuitive response to Nick made her wonder how far she would take this thing if he really pressed her.

"I had a run-in with a nasty character," she finally told him, her words taut.

His arm tightened around her back. "You were mugged for your purse in Central Park or something?" He sounded as if he might really care.

"Something."

Tension vibrated between them, but thankfully Nick left it alone. Memories of the incident still vivid, Sasha sank into silence herself until they'd ascended to the penthouse level and left the elevator.

"So how many big-time spenders are going to line the house's pockets tonight?" she asked, giving his penthouse entrance a quick inspection as they passed it. Indeed, the door was equipped with a dead bolt.

"Four. Harry Conley, Karen Fuller, Quin Reardon and Gaines VanDerZanden. Maybe some of the names are familiar."

Karen Fuller and Quin Reardon were Hollywood types whose stars had faded nearly a decade before, Sasha knew. Harry Conley was a well-known tennis bum, who'd blown his chance at the Olympics. But she wasn't familiar with Gaines VanDerZanden—probably some wealthy executive.

"Quite a lineup," she murmured.

"We try."

Not into gambling—at least not this kind—Sasha didn't quite get the allure. Oh, she could probably unload a roll of quarters into a slot machine without blinking an eye, and she'd had a blast shooting craps once in Atlantic City, where she'd won a whole twenty bucks. But high rollers in a private game meant big-time money. The line dividing gambling as entertainment from gambling as trouble was a thin one.

Still, she was passing no judgments on anyone as she entered the presidential suite. Her mind was elsewhere, back on the entrance to Nick's penthouse.

The question was: How could she sneak away from the gathering long enough to get inside his place and search it?

VITO TOLENTINO covered his surprise when Nick arrived with the leggy new show girl on his arm. While the boss nibbled through the chorus line like a mouse went through cheese, he normally kept his women separate from his business. In charge of security for all private games, Vito held the station at the bar, not too far from the entryway, while his assistant perched on a stool in the opposite corner.

Nick settled the Brozynski dame on a stool and moved closer to him. "How's it going?"

"Smooth," Vito answered in a low voice. "Everybody's happy."

"Schneider doing a good job?"

"I got no complaints."

"Good."

Vito checked his watch. "Break's coming up in a few minutes."

"Then we timed our arrival just right."

Glancing over at Nick's latest, Vito realized the show girl didn't seem too interested in the play around the table. Odd, considering the identities of the well-known players. Instead, she was looking the place over like she was checking the layout or something. His sharply honed instincts had seen Vito through some rough times over the years and right now alarms were trumpeting inside his head.

Sasha Brozynski was no dumb bimbo. And she was a friend of JoJo Weston's. Even though he'd brought her to the boss himself, Vito was surprised Nick had hired her knowing that. Nick had said he'd hired her *because* of it.

Having worked for the Donatellis all his life—ever since the old man had picked him up out of a gutter at the age of thirteen—and having played nursemaid to all three kids at one time or another, he should understand Nick's thinking.

Only he didn't, at least not this time.

JoJo had been some piece of work, making everyone think she was a dame with class....

If Sasha Brozynski planned on stepping into her friend's dancing shoes, she was definitely trouble.

And Vito didn't like trouble.

Trouble made him sweat inside.

If the Brozynski dame proved him right, she would rue the day she'd danced her way into the Caribbean.

Vito would see to making things right, like he always did for the Donatelli family.

SASHA WAS RELIEVED when a break was called. The way Vito Tolentino was glaring at her—almost like he had figured out what she was up to—made her edgy.

"Ah, Donatelli, there you are!" roared Gaines VanDerZanden, who turned out to be a silver-haired fashion plate. "I thought you weren't going to show."

"Would I let you roll into town without giving you my personal welcome?"

"No, of course not. And who is this stunning creature?"

"My newest show girl. Sasha Brozynski."

A wicked gleam in his piercing blue eyes, Gaines took her hand and, in continental fashion, raised it to his mouth. He let his lips linger against her skin a bit too long, and Sasha found herself pulling her hand free.

"Nice to meet you."

"The pleasure is all mine." He turned to Nick. "Changed your mind about the redhead, eh?"

"JoJo took off," Nick returned. "She had bigger fish to fry."

Gaines indicated Sasha. "I assume she's yours, then."

Stunned by his rudeness, not to mention the callous reference about JoJo, Sasha didn't think before she spoke. "Excuse me, but I'm a person here, not an object. I belong to myself. If you want to know whether or not I'm attached, then you talk to me."

Silver brows raised, he asked, "Are you?"

"I haven't decided, yet." She felt Nick's gaze bore into her and figured he'd have a few things to say to her later about upsetting one of his best customers. She tried to smooth things over. "But I'm flattered that you asked."

"Perhaps I'll ask again in the near future. If that's all right with you."

"Sure. A little flattery never hurts a girl's ego."

Now she was really feeling weird. Thankfully, Nick changed the subject and the two men did some catching up on mutual acquaintances. She breathed a sigh of relief and slid across the room, knowing all the while that Vito Tolentino was keeping an eye on her. Great. If she tried to make her move, would it be under his eye?

She was checking the layout of the suite around the entryway hall and realized the powder room was around the corner, out of view of the parlor. And the way things were set up inside, only one or two of the players could actually get a clear shot of the door—and only if they didn't have something more important to concentrate on.

She was concentrating on her plan when she realized she had yet another man's interest. The dealer was standing a bare yard away, sipping a cola, his dark-brown eyes riveted to her every movement. The same dealer who'd been in Nick's penthouse the day before. And the same dealer who'd posed for a photo with Barbie and JoJo.

Thinking he might be able to give her some information about her missing friend, she flashed him a smile. In return, he saluted her with his glass of soda.

"Sasha, right? I heard you tell old VanDerZanden off," he said so quietly she had to strain to hear. "Good for you. The guy thinks the world revolves around him. I just hope it didn't lose you your job."

She grimaced. "You think Nick . . . uh, Mr. D . . . will fire me for standing up for myself?"

He shrugged and sipped his soda. "Hard to tell. You never know what Donatelli might do when he's crossed. He can be unpredictable."

The way he said it gave her goose bumps. "Sounds like you know him real well."

"Well enough."

Well enough not to like Nick, she was certain of that. "What did you say your name was?"

"Mac Schneider. I usually deal blackjack."

"Nice to know another employee—one who isn't a dancer."

"Maybe we can get to know one another better."

The opening she'd been waiting for. But how could she see another man while trying to make Nick fall for her? Torn, she hesitated. "Well—"

"As friendly co-employees," he quickly put in. "Our having a cup of coffee together shouldn't put anyone's nose out of joint, right?"

She glanced at Nick, who seemed to be focused on his customer. And, yet, she had the distinct feeling he knew her every move. "Yeah, right. Why not."

"Tomorrow?"

"I'm rehearsing all day."

"You have to take a breather sometime. Say about three-thirty?"

Not wanting to lose the opportunity, she made up her mind. "Three-thirty it is." She'd square it with Yale somehow.

Mac was grinning at her, and Sasha realized he had his own brand of charisma in addition to good looks. He was as tall as she, and his medium build was trim and muscled. The features that went with the dark eyes and hair were just short of handsome.

Not that he was in Nick's league...any woman would describe Nick Donatelli as *drop-dead gorgeous*. And intense. Certainly exciting. Possibly hazardous to a girl's heart rate, if not her health. Then again, that had nothing to do with looks. What Nick also had was an aura of power that drew attention to him like a magnet to steel.

"I'll meet you at the Sandbar," Mac was saying. "That's the coffee shop." He checked his watch. "Uh-oh, break time's almost up."

Winking at her playfully, the dealer returned to the table where three of the players were already seated.

And over at the bar, Gaines VanDerZanden was still bending Nick's ear.

"Game time," Vito called.

Gaines broke away from Nick, who immediately turned his full attention on Sasha. A thrill swept through her, and Sasha told herself the strange sensation was due to her nervousness over her immediate plan. She mouthed the words "ladies' room" and pointed in the direction of the powder room. He nodded and settled back against the bar near Vito, his gaze settling on the game that was already resuming.

Sasha rounded the corner, then paused to listen to cards being shuffled and chips being thrown into the pot. Under cover of the swell of voices, she tiptoed back to the suite door and opened it silently, all the while keeping an eye on those who could see her if they looked this way—Mac and the two film stars. But as far as she could tell, all attention was focused on the game.

As she slipped through the doorway, she rotated the handle and released the door's latch, so that she would be able to reenter at will. Once in the hall, she eased the door closed behind her and hurried toward Nick's penthouse, her hand already inside her bag to retrieve the key.

Seconds later, standing in front of his door, she took a deep breath. This was it. Her chance to find out what happened to JoJo. What would Nick do if he caught her inside?

He'd want to know how she got his key and why she was using it. If he figured out the truth...

The possibility made her heart pound wildly.

She produced the key. Her hand shook slightly as she aimed it at the door. Adrenaline shot through her when she couldn't immediately insert the damned thing. Her nerves were getting to her. She tried again. But no amount of wiggling would get the key into that lock.

It simply didn't fit.

Sasha palmed the metal and mulled over the ramifications of that fact. She wanted to feel relieved ... and she did to some extent. Though the key not fitting Nick's lock didn't mean he hadn't been responsible for her friend's disappearance. She realized that was wishful thinking.

"What the hell are you up to?" came a masculine growl behind her, causing Sasha to nearly jump out of her skin.

Whirling around, facing a glower that would scare the bananas out of a gorilla, she thought fast. Smiled. "Oh, there you are, Nicky," she cooed, covertly slipping the key back into her bag. "When I came out of the ladies' room, I didn't see you, so I figured you must have come back to your place to get something. I was simply looking for you."

Though he didn't appear any less suspicious, he said, "I only left the game now."

"I guess I just didn't look good enough," she said as innocently as she could manage.

She didn't think he believed her, but he let the lie go. Smiling inside and out with relief, she took a step back toward the game ... and plunged directly into the wall of his chest as he stepped in front of her.

Nerves tingling, blood rushing, she cocked her head and stared directly into Nick's feral grin.

Wondering what the dazzling liar had been up to, Nick said, "I wouldn't want to disappoint you."

"I'm not disappointed."

But she was nervous. A tick at the corner of one otherwise flawless amber eye betrayed her.

"If you want into my place," he said magnani-
mously, "far be it from me to deny you."

Purposefully, he pulled his key ring from his pocket
and reached past her.

Her hand on his wrist stopped him. "No, really," she
protested, her breath coming quickly. "I don't want to
take you away from your game."

"I was ready to take a hike, anyway."

"Oh."

Check and mate. He had her. He could back her into
a very comfortable corner—his apartment—if he so
chose. Certain she would go along with him rather than
protest, even when she so obviously didn't want to, Nick
couldn't help but wonder why. He also wondered how
far she would go to further this masquerade of hers.

Imagining how far he'd like to take her—how she
would feel slipping under him and over him, rolling
naked with him over the satin sheets covering his king-
size bed—he had an urge to push and find out for certain.

He slipped an arm around her waist, slowly, so that
she wouldn't freak. Knowing that she'd been attacked
or "something," as she'd admitted earlier, explained
why she'd hauled off and cracked him when he'd scared
her the night before.

The lady ain't seen nothing yet, he thought. He could
scare her like she'd never been scared before....

"So what do you say?" he murmured.

Her eyes clouding over, she seemed a bit confused.
"About what?"

"About this."

He kissed her as he'd been wanting to all night. The
peck he'd given her backstage had merely fueled his
hunger. She was ripe, all right, and her juices were

flowing... right into his mouth... against his body... flooding his senses... making him want to take her on the spot. He smoothly moved his hand up to cup the fullness of her breast. She made a small sound at the back of her throat that threatened to send him straight over the edge.

He should take her with him. He really should. He disliked women who thought they could pull something on him. Women who gave him too little credit.

So why didn't he dislike her?

And why did he choose to let her off the hook?

He loosened his hold. Maybe it was because she was an amateur. Maybe because some other man had already taught her a lesson that she didn't deserve. The question of exactly what had happened to keep her from working bugged him. But he'd get an answer.

And eventually he'd get her.

Like Vito said, he always got what he wanted one way or another.

He brushed a thumb across her cheek, smoothed her wild-woman hair away from her face with the back of his hand. "So let's go down to the Coral Reef Bar for a nightcap."

"Let's," she agreed, relief written all over her face as clear as an advertisement.

He slid an arm around her waist and guided her to the elevator. He could wait. For now.

REPRIEVE. The word rolled around in Sasha's head as the elevator shot down toward the ground floor. Nick had sorely tested her, though. When he'd kissed her, her mind had leapfrogged ahead and she'd seen them together... inside his apartment... in a much more intimate embrace.

Feeling yet another flush climb over her skin, she tried to get her mind off the subject. "So, Gaines VanDerZanden knew JoJo?"

"He'd met her a few times."

"But he didn't like her?"

"To the contrary. He thought he could buy her away from me."

Sasha started at Nick's amused tone. Was he really that smug that he figured there was no contest if he was in the competition? She could hardly believe the extent of his arrogance.

"So, was JoJo interested?"

"In Gaines? He wasn't any woman's prospective groom, if that's what you're fishing for."

Her mouth went dry. She hadn't told him about the aborted wedding. Casually, Nick reached out and hit a red button that brought the elevator car to an immediate stop. But Sasha's stomach went plummeting. She backed away from him, toward the opposite side of the car.

"You knew?"

"That JoJo was planning on getting married? No, not all along. That you flew here so you could be maid of honor?" Nick's expression held censure that frightened her. "Don't think you can keep secrets from me, Sasha," he said, moving closer. "I have eyes and ears everywhere."

And people who would keep *his* secrets, like covering up for him should *she* disappear just like JoJo, Sasha thought, fighting panic. Panicking would get her nothing but more hurt as she knew from experience.

Still, she couldn't help the surge of her heartbeat as she gauged the distance to the button that would release the car. Or the knot that tied up her stomach as she tried to calculate whether or not she could get there before him.

"Don't even think about it."

She tried anyway, and for her efforts was stopped cold as he shoved himself between her and the panel. Her response to the threat was instinctive and automatic. She took a defensive stance, shoulder on an angle to him, hands up between them, just as she'd practiced over and over and over in past months.

"Keep away from me!" she ordered.

But Nick wasn't moving so much as a toe in her direction. He didn't even appear in the least concerned. His gaze held hers steadily.

"You surprised me once," he admitted. "That won't happen again. And all the lessons in self-defense you could ever take won't protect you from *me*." His threat sounded both dangerous and seductive. "I thought you should know what you're up against if you're going to continue playing this game of yours."

She relaxed her position slightly, but not her attention. "What game?"

"The one where you pretend to come on to me when you really don't want to."

Lord, had he seen through everything from the first? "With your arrogance, I would have thought my attraction to you would be totally believable."

"Oh, I do believe it. Just as I know I'm the last man on earth you would choose to be attracted to. You just can't help yourself."

She sputtered, "Why you arrogant—"

"So while you don't want to be attracted to me," he went on, "you really are, and so the pretense isn't really pretense…I guess." His brow furrowed. "I'll have to think about that one." He shook his head, chasing away the confused expression. "You may be one of the hottest dancers I've ever had the pleasure to watch, Sasha, but your acting technique could use some work."

With that, she dropped her arms and collapsed against the wall. Had she really been all that transparent? Or did Nick know women so well that he could see right through them?

"What now?" she asked.

He reached over and released the button. The elevator car dropped as fast as her heart when she realized Nick would probably fire her and she might never have the chance to learn her friend's fate.

"Now we go have that drink."

"I'm not thirsty."

"Sulking?"

Sasha didn't answer, merely tried to get herself together before the elevator doors opened. Nick took her arm and ignored the fact that she stiffened at his touch. He guided her toward the Coral Reef Bar, past Lester Perkins, who was cleaning up a spill. The maintenance man stared after them in a way that sent a chill shooting up Sasha's spine.

"He seems awfully interested in us," she murmured.

"Poor bastard. I feel sorry for him. He goes around mooning over show girls instead of finding a flesh-and-blood woman who would appreciate him."

Realizing he was serious, Sasha melted a little. Maybe Nick Donatelli had a heart beneath all that arrogance. A heart that had been betrayed by three women . . . two of whom were dead. She didn't want to think that JoJo was, too.

As they swept by the bartender, Nick ordered them beers with lime—no mescal, thank goodness—and herded her into the only empty booth, which just happened to be in a dark corner.

They were barely seated, drinks appearing like magic, when he asked, "If you wanted to know about me and JoJo, why didn't you just ask?"

"Would you have told me?"

"Try it and see."

"All right. What about you and JoJo?" Boldly, she continued, "Exactly how close were you?"

"I never slept with her."

The knot that had settled in the middle of her stomach untied. An unexpected reaction to an unexpected response. "And I'm supposed to believe that?"

"Yes. What else?"

As she squeezed the juice from a wedge of lime into her beer mug, she gauged Nick's sincerity. Could it really be? A man of his obvious appetites passing on a dish like JoJo?

Realizing he was waiting, she went on. "Did you ask her to marry you?"

Throwing back his head, Nick laughed. "Way off base. I only asked a woman to marry me once, years ago, and that's a mistake I don't intend to repeat."

Why that statement should bother her was a mystery. He had to be referring to Mia Scudella, who'd broken off the engagement for some unknown reason. Surely that experience hadn't soured him on all women. But having gotten the idea that he went through women like a slot-machine player went through quarters, Sasha figured it just might have soured him. She sipped at her lime-flavored beer.

"Do you know who JoJo was supposed to marry?" Sasha asked.

"Not a clue."

"What about why she disappeared?"

He was silent for a moment, then said, "That's complicated."

Her pulse began to tick. "How so?"

"You won't like it."

Thinking she was getting somewhere at last, Sasha sat forward, leaning halfway across the table. "Try me."

"JoJo Weston's a thief."

"What?" Automatically coming to her friend's defense, she said, "JoJo wouldn't take anyone's money."

"I never said money."

The denial stopped her cold. Sasha frowned at Nick. "For heaven's sake, what, then?"

"Like I said, it's complicated."

"And you're not going to tell me."

"Not today."

Did that mean he would tell her another day if she kept after him? Suspicious, wondering if this wasn't a ploy, a game he meant to play with her to get even for her jerking his strings, she sat back against the cushioned surface and took his measure as he downed half his beer.

Nick Donatelli was a complex man. Dangerous. Frightening. Seductive. A lethal combination.

"My turn."

"Your turn to what?"

"Ask the questions. And I expect you to be as honest with me as I have been with you."

"Fair enough."

"If JoJo hadn't disappeared, would you have asked me for work, anyway?"

"Maybe. JoJo'd been bugging me about trying out Las Vegas."

"So you took the job for the express purpose of what?"

"I figured I might as well wait around until I found out what happened to her."

"Which you imagine is what?"

Not wanting to present her worst-case scenario, especially since it involved him, Sasha merely shrugged.

"I thought you were going to be honest."

"I am being as honest with you as you were with me," she countered. "When you tell me what JoJo supposedly stole from you, I'll elaborate."

Sasha could tell from Nick's expression that she didn't have to. That he knew. And that he was angry with her. For believing a lie? Or for knowing the truth?

She shuddered inside and tried to cover by guzzling her beer. She shouldn't get too comfortable with Nick, should maybe stay away from him at all costs.

And to that end, when she called it a night and he followed her out of the bar, offering to walk her to her car, she said, "I don't need your brand of protection." Protection that made her vulnerable.

He didn't try to change her mind, merely stood in the same spot and called after her, "We'll pick up where we left off tomorrow."

Pick up what? The conversation about JoJo? Or something more personal?

The inadvisability of letting Nick get too close was clear to Sasha. As was the temptation. The fact that he was dangerous didn't dampen her attraction to him. Maybe it even fueled Nick's appeal for her. She couldn't remember ever meeting another man who was her match.

She mentally debated the issue all the way to the car and halfway home, as well. Only when she could see the apartment complex drawing closer did Sasha's thoughts turn more directly to her friend. Was she a fool to think she could find JoJo? What next? Would she get anything more out of Nick?

Thinking she'd better sweeten her chances by making friends and influencing people, she vowed to start with Mac the next afternoon. She would even work on Barbie. Of course she wouldn't see the other show girl for yet another day. And every day that JoJo was gone...

Sasha left the car in a slot, realizing the complex lights had gone off in the time it had taken her to park. Careful of her footing, she made her way slowly across the grounds, a few lit apartments guiding her, and her nose heading her toward the chemically treated swimming pool.

A swish of the brush nearby made her think she'd interrupted some animal's nocturnal wanderings. Realizing she hadn't seen any of the high desert wildlife, yet, she flashed around to get a look, but the moon was under cloud cover and seeing was impossible. All she could make out were dark silhouettes of cars and buildings and palm trees.

Shaking away an uneasy feeling that she put down to nerves, she went on, thinking that tomorrow afternoon would be forty-eight hours. The police would do something then. But what? Other than telling her to stop interfering with their job. She wasn't about to stop, and they could mess things up for her more than she had already done herself. Besides which, she didn't believe for one moment the authorities would really care about a missing show girl who had supposedly been getting married—especially when there was no evidence of foul play.

But she cared, damn it! She wasn't going to let it go. She'd have to make that report to a bunch of bureaucrats, who probably wouldn't do anything unless she found something tangible to convince them there was something to investigate.

A scuffling from somewhere behind her startled Sasha. Again, searching for its source in the near dark was a waste of time. This sound could have been made by clumsy feet rather than an animal...making her question the first one she'd heard.

Surely she hadn't interrupted a prowler....

Or had she?

Wariness lent her speed, and she cursed the fact that JoJo's building had to be the most isolated in the complex. Then a subtle rustling between her and the building made her veer off in another direction. Whoever was creeping around the grounds was not trying to stay out of her way. Her senses heightened, and when she placed furtive movement behind her, the hair rose on the back of her neck.

Someone was trying to frighten her and was doing a damn fine job of it, too.

She knew the rules like a mantra. The first line of self-defense was to avoid being selected as a target. She'd purposely made herself one, even if she hadn't had the opportunity to carry out her plan. Nick had seen right through her. But had he figured out everything?

Was Nick Donatelli stalking her?

Furious at the possibility, she was tempted to stop and face him, to tell him what she thought of his maneuvering. To make enough noise to force him to back off. But what if she screamed and no one heard? The hour was late and the occupants of the complex were most certainly in bed. And what if Nick really was not only physically dangerous but willing to risk everything long enough to finish what he'd come for?

What if he was a killer as the tabloids had implied?

Nearing the swimming pool once more, she slipped off her shoes and ran as fast and as soundlessly as she could. Something clattered behind her. She raced onto a strip of desert grass, harsh against her stockinged feet, and ducked low, hoping the foliage would hide her flight as she changed directions once again. She sought shelter in the shadow of the nearest building, racing around the soda machine and ice maker, plastering herself against the stucco wall, praying she could make herself invisible.

She gripped her shoes hard, one in each hand, thinking she could use them as weapons if need be, though she had plenty of her own—hands, feet, fingers, knees, teeth. She took deep, calming breaths, stilling her mind, preparing herself for what she might have to do.

Her mouth was dry, while the sweat of fear dribbled down her back and between her breasts.

She *could* do this. Could protect herself. She'd been hurt before and survived. Survival was the key word. And now she knew how to hurt back. Only she'd never had to before. She'd never wanted to. She still didn't.

Minutes passed. Then blocks of time with no repeat of the stealthy noises that had panicked her. She relaxed a bit, but still she could not force herself to move from her safe spot. Could not force herself to test her new skills.

So she waited.

Her legs grew shaky and she fought fatigue. She had to stay alert....

Suddenly, Sasha was flooded in bright light as the fixtures around the complex popped on all at once. Had he found the breaker box? Had he turned out the lights in the first place, and now put them back on in his determination to find her at all costs?

Her worst fear was confirmed when footsteps approached from the back of the building. She jumped away from the wall and prepared to fight for her life.

The man who rounded the corner was as startled to see her as she was to see him. Thin and stooped, probably in his seventies, he was dressed in pajamas and slippers and carrying a flashlight in one hand, a big key ring in the other.

"Who the hell are you?" he demanded.

Sasha realized he must be the owner or at least the maintenance man. "The building in back—apartment 2C."

He squinted. "You ain't Miss Weston. She has red hair. And she's shorter."

"I'm a friend of JoJo's. I'm staying in her place while she's away."

"Casper Johnson, owner of this oasis in the desert." He squinted as if he needed glasses that he wasn't wearing. "So what're you doing wandering around out here in the middle of the night?"

"There was a prowler. He did something to the lights..."

"Nah, no one did nothing to the lights!" He waved a hand at her. "The missus got me up to turn them back on. The box was still locked. Musta been a surge that triggered the breaker. Happens once in a while."

"But I'm sure someone was out there."

"Animals, probably, coming for water from the pool. Loaded with chemicals but they drink the water, anyway."

That's what she'd thought at first. But a person had been out there. Right? Surely she hadn't imagined the whole thing.

"You look a mite nervous. You want some company back to your building?"

Sasha sagged with relief. "Thanks. I'd appreciate it."

But she didn't let up her guard. Her gaze skimmed the grounds, now bathed in golden light. Nothing out of place. No movement. No sound.

Of course, he'd had time to get away clean.

He. Nick Donatelli? What if Nick hadn't been the one? What if it had been someone else? Someone innocent in intent? Or an animal, just as Mr. Johnson had maintained. Maybe her nerves hadn't recovered as well as she'd thought.

At the foot of the stairs leading to the second floor, Sasha smiled at Mr. Johnson. "Thanks. I can take it from here."

"Always pleased to escort a pretty lady. You let that imagination of yours rest now."

"Sure thing."

She only hoped she could live up to her confident words and find release in sleep.

Chapter Six

Mac Schneider felt as if he were wearing a hole in the carpeting, pacing back and forth in front of the coffee shop. He checked his watch for the tenth time. Three-thirty-eight. Damn! She wasn't going to show.

He figured he had time before his shift, so he might as well wait awhile longer. Fists jammed into his pockets, fingers jingling the keys in one, change in the other, he rocked on his heels and gazed around the casino. Several more minutes passed. Just when he was about to call it a lost cause, he spotted Sasha Brozynski, her long legs eating the distance as she practically jogged through the late-afternoon crowd.

Stopping a yard before him, she took a big breath. "Sorry I'm late."

Not that she sounded contrite. And Mac didn't like being kept waiting. He covered his true annoyance.

He said, "No problem," punctuating his acceptance of her apology with a winning smile. He could be just as insincere as she. "My shift doesn't start until five, anyway. I have lots of time."

She grimaced. "While I have to be back on stage in twenty minutes."

He'd been hoping for more, but he'd take what he could get. "Let's order that coffee, then."

Besides, once he turned on the charm, he could probably convince her to be late if necessary. Or make another assignation....

Because it was early and the Sandbar was nearly empty, they were seated immediately and the waitress quickly brought their coffees.

Mac gave Sasha his most charming smile. "So, how's it going?" he asked, stirring several packets of sugar into his mug to make the stuff inside palatable. "With the rehearsals, I mean?"

"Pretty smooth. Starting tomorrow night, I'll be in the opening and close with everyone else. Plus, I'll be doing a spot with Lance...oh, Lord, I forget his last name."

"Anderson," he supplied. "Barbie mentioned it."

She sipped at her coffee and asked, "Oh, are you and Barbie friends? Not that I'm trying to pry."

He started, but her expression spelled innocence. He was being paranoid. Not that paranoid was a bad thing. It had probably saved his butt more than once. Maybe she *was* interested in him, but was the type of woman who didn't step into another's territory.

"Barbie and I know each other pretty well," he said, sipping his coffee. Still not sweet enough. He stirred in another packet. "We went out a few times."

"Nothing serious."

"Right. Just two friends doing the town together."

"You must be in heaven with so many show girls to pick from."

"I don't know that many."

"How about JoJo Weston?"

Wondering if this was more than simple curiosity, if she could possibly know anything concrete, he asked, "What about her?"

"You know her, right?"

"We've met."

"I wish *I* could meet up with her." Sasha stared into her mug. "We were friends in New York and she kept trying to get me to come out here ever since she moved."

"So you finally did and she took a powder on you, huh?"

"Something like that." Her gaze met his. "Actually, I thought I was going to her wedding, only the bride and groom didn't show. Didn't Barbie tell you?"

Mac played dumb. "Barbie doesn't tell me everything. So who was this guy—the groom, I mean."

"I was hoping *you* might know."

He laughed. "The Caribbean is a big place. Probably lots of real-life soap operas being played out. It would be hard to keep up."

"No doubt."

Mac could tell the answer didn't satisfy her. Too bad. She wouldn't recognize the truth if it hit her square between the eyes, anyway. Look at the way she was hanging all over Donatelli.

"Speaking of friends...are you and Mr. D an item?" he asked, trying to make the question sound casual.

"I haven't even dated him."

"That's not an answer."

Sasha was slow to give him one. Finally, she said, "Nicky does have his charms, but I'm not committed to them."

"And you shouldn't be."

"Why not?"

"Some girls who get involved with Donatelli get in serious trouble," Mac said. "I'd hate for you to be one of them."

"I'll keep that in mind."

Again, the charming smile. "I'd like to see you again. Maybe I can save you from yourself."

She laughed. "My hero."

"No, I'm serious." He scowled as he thought about it. "Nick Donatelli isn't a man to fool around with. He's done things . . ."

"Nothing he's been convicted of."

"That doesn't mean he's innocent," Mac said, unable to keep the rancor from his tone. "Only that he hasn't been prosecuted because he has the right connections. You know who his father is, don't you?"

"I've heard. And his father served time."

"There you go."

"That doesn't prove anything," Sasha said reasonably. "If Salvatore Donatelli had that much influence in the right places, he wouldn't have served time himself. Besides, I don't judge anyone because of family connections. Or because of rumor and speculation. I figure everyone deserves a chance to prove himself."

"Just don't give Donatelli too big a chance or you might not live to be sorry," Mac warned her.

If Sasha was taken in by that gangster, he thought sourly, she deserved what she would end up getting.

"I DON'T KNOW WHAT I did with my cellular phone," Yale complained at rehearsal's end. He was checking behind the seats.

"Did you have it when you were checking set pieces?" Sasha thought of the lower levels below the stage where sets and props were stored, and from where performers made grand entrances.

"You're right. I don't have time to look for it now. I'm late. And speaking of late...try not to be tomorrow."

She flashed him a smile but made no promises that she might break. Even when she put forth her best effort, she was always a step behind.

Like with Mac Schneider.

Her dissatisfying discussion with him rolling over and over in her head, she made her way to the deserted dressing room and her assigned locker. After changing into a calf-length, brightly patterned gauze skirt and a sleeveless teal top, she stuffed her rehearsal clothes into her shoulder bag, then whipped out a wide-tooth comb to deal with her hair.

Why did she get the feeling that Mac knew something he wasn't saying? And that, while he professed interest in her, he wasn't the least bit attracted?

Odd. Probably what had prompted her to agree that she'd enjoy spending some time with him in the near future. She'd sensed he was charged just below his calm surface, and she wanted to know what was jolting his batteries. Besides, something told her he hadn't exactly been forthcoming about JoJo.

Preoccupied as she made her way out of the showroom, Sasha wasn't paying attention to her surroundings and so nearly walked right into a gold-and-purple flower-printed chest.

"Nicky." She backed off, feeling awkward. "What are you doing here?"

He stared down at her from hooded eyes. "I own the place, remember."

Also remembering Mac's warning on top of the incident at the apartment complex the night before, she felt a chill slide up her spine.

"Rehearsal went well," she told him. "Yale says I'm ready to go on tomorrow night. I don't have to be back until five for a run-through."

"Good. Then you can stay up as late as you want."

"I could if I had a reason." She started to swing by him, but was stopped when he startled her by, yet again, grabbing her upper arm.

"You do."

Sasha stared down at the hand that detained her, as if she could force Nick to let go through sheer will. Her heart pounded with a combination of fear and attraction when the hand stayed put. She felt each individual finger as if they were imprinted on her skin. Sasha steeled her mind from wandering into more dangerous territory.

She could stop herself from responding to him even if she couldn't stop herself from wanting to.

"Do you have to grab every woman you know?" she demanded. "Or is it just me?"

"Every woman doesn't keep trying to get away." His smile was aloof, almost mocking. "In some circles, I'm actually sought after."

"Good for you. Can I go now?"

He let go. "You have to eat."

"I'm capable of feeding myself, Nick."

"What happened to Nicky?"

"What?"

"Your calling me Nicky might annoy the hell out of me," he admitted with a scowl, "but I get the feeling you mean it despite yourself."

She was feeling a lot of things despite herself. Despite her good sense. She *wanted* to be with him, and not just for JoJo. She'd told Mac she judged a person for himself and not because of family or rumor or speculation. But if she cut Nick off without giving him a fair chance, wasn't that exactly what she was doing?

Sasha forced herself to relax. Forced herself to say, "Yeah, I do have to eat, Nicky. So what do you have in mind?"

That transformed his face from grim to grin. And, for the moment, Sasha was lost.

"I thought we could eat at *Donatelli's*."

"You want to take me home for dinner?"

"No, *Donatelli's* is the family restaurant. Though you would have to put up with my father and kid sister. Caroline's been on my case for ignoring them."

"And you want me to go along?"

The last thing any ordinary man would want of a woman he didn't know well, lest the family members get the wrong idea about the seriousness of the relationship. Not that Nick was in any way ordinary. And maybe he had his own reasons for not wanting to be alone with them.

"Why not?" he demanded.

Why not, indeed. The outing would give her the opportunity to see Nick in a different setting. Get a feel for what he was like away from the Caribbean. Get a feel for exactly how close he was with his family, especially with his father—hardened criminal that Sally Donatelli was.

"Sure," she finally agreed. "I'll be your protection."

His thick brows slashed upward at that one, but he didn't deny it. "You like Italian?"

Gazing at him, she said, "Given the chance, I might even be crazy about it." Then, realizing what the admission sounded like, she hurriedly added, "Uh, but I have to change first."

"What's wrong with what you're wearing?"

Nick was intently studying the way the thin skirt material clung to her hips and thighs. Not exactly appropriate wear for a nice restaurant—or a family meeting.

"I haven't exactly been standing still all day. I'd like to wash the grime off. Give me the address and I'll meet you there," she suggested.

"How about I follow you to your place and wait for you to change."

Did he think she wouldn't show? "You know the place well enough to get there yourself," she said, moving through the casino.

Following closely, making every inch of her aware of him, Nick murmured, "And where would that be?"

Was he kidding or what? Near the blackjack tables, she stopped and stared at Nick's unclouded expression. If he didn't know, that meant he hadn't followed her the night before. Or that he was a better actor than she was.

"For now, I'm bunked in JoJo's apartment," Sasha said, shutting out the sounds and movement around her and focusing on his reaction.

Nick's jaw tightened as if, indeed, he hadn't a clue—and as if he were displeased by the information. Sasha felt a tiny bit of relief.

And yet...

"I figured you knew," she said, unable to stop herself from pushing it.

"What made you figure that?"

She took a big breath and said, "When I left here last night, you followed me home, didn't you?" She couldn't be any more direct than that.

His gaze changed subtly. "Last night, I never left the hotel. You certain your imagination wasn't running wild because you *wanted* me to be around?"

Mr. Johnson had made a similar claim about her imagination, but Nick's assumption was downright arrogant.

"I hardly ever let any part of me run wild," she insisted, placing a restraining hand on his chest when he tried to get closer. "Not even my imagination."

His brows shot up at that one. "Really?"

And she knew he was looking to steer the conversation in a direction that would effectively distract her. She wouldn't have it. She was going to get this thing in the open, and let the chips fall where they may. When someone tried to get past her to approach one of the blackjack tables, she held her ground, not even glancing at the person who had to skirt around them.

"Someone either followed me home last night, Nicky, or was waiting for me to arrive. Whoever it was scared the bejeezus out of me, slinking around the grounds in the dark."

His suddenly intense expression made her heart pound.

"You're sure about this?"

"So if it wasn't you," she continued obstinately, "then who?"

Nick hesitated only a second before saying, "I don't have a clue."

His hesitation gave Sasha the impression that maybe he did have a clue—one he didn't like. That would mean he, himself, was innocent of any wrongdoing. She wanted to believe him, so she gave him the benefit of the doubt.

Nodding, she said, "We'd better get going." She turned to find Mac Schneider working the closest blackjack table even while he was staring at them.

When their gazes locked, Mac quickly glanced away toward his customers. Sasha wondered if Nick had noticed his interest . . . and if Mac had picked up any part of their conversation. Neither she nor Nick had made an effort to control the volume.

Shaking away the discomfort the idea of Mac's knowing her business generated, she proceeded to the parking lot, Nick uncomfortably close at her side.

They took separate cars, and she noticed he didn't let hers out of sight. She wondered if he would let *her* out of sight long enough to dress. The idea of him watching her strip made her clutch inside. Fantasies teased her whether she would or no. More was going on between them than she was comfortable with, that was for certain.

But when they got to JoJo's apartment, Nick immediately sprawled in a chair and picked up the television remote. "I'll watch the tube while you change."

Rather, he began channel surfing, Sasha noted. Some things about the male animal seemed to be universal. Her gaze lingered on Nick awhile longer as he worked the remote. He seemed perfectly at home. How many times had he taken over the television while waiting for JoJo?

The thought troubled her as she climbed out of her clothes and hit the shower. Nick had vowed he hadn't slept with her friend, but could she believe him? She hadn't a clue. Not about anything.

Maybe she should relax already and see where things went. Pretend she was just going on a first date.

First date.

Now that made her feel weird.

They'd already kissed more than once. She'd already had erotic fantasies about the man. She felt as if she and Nick had been playing games with each other for a long time rather than two measly days. She felt as if he might know her too well. Like he was already under her skin. . . .

Thinking to protect herself against him by dressing conservatively, Sasha was at a loss as to how she might accomplish that. She normally put herself right out there, had the moxie to carry off hot new fashions without blinking her false eyelashes. Conservative wasn't part of her wardrobe.

But it was part of JoJo's.

Though Sasha knew she was a size larger than her friend, JoJo usually liked to wear loose clothing and often bought garments a size bigger than she really needed. They'd often borrowed from each other when they'd been roommates, just about doubling their individual wardrobes. She didn't think JoJo would mind, wherever she might be, if Sasha did so now.

So she delved into JoJo's closet, coming out with a plain black sheath that fit her like a second skin. The neckline was high, but the skirt came only to mid-thigh. Thinking to fix that problem, she added a pair of her own Lycra footless tights and black flats.

Satisfied that the dress now looked like a tunic, she delved into her friend's jewelry box and grabbed the pearls she'd noticed before. After slicking her hair away from her face and securing it back with a big black bow, she added the unusual pearl choker with its front clasp of jet beads. A light application of makeup and she was ready.

And Nick was expecting her, television off, staring as she shot through the bedroom door. Had he been sitting there, visualizing her in the altogether? His expression was certainly appreciative.

Embarrassed at her own reaction to the way her imagination went cruising, Sasha covered by turning away, heading toward the door and demanding, "So what are you waiting for?"

"For my pulse to steady," he said. "If I get up too fast, I might get dizzy."

A hot flush spread through her. She gave him an annoyed look. "C'mon."

Then he was right behind her, so close that she could feel his body heat. Glad to be in the open, busying herself locking the door, she was thankful they wouldn't be dining alone. She didn't trust herself, not to mention him.

"So what time are they expecting us? Or you, rather?"

"Right now."

"Why didn't you tell me?"

"And make you more nervous?"

"I am not nervous."

"Liar."

Because he was correct, she didn't argue, merely allowed him to lead her to his red convertible. Always crazy about old cars, she recognized the restored '68 Corvette Mako Shark with chrome pipes and a spotless white leather interior. The equally white top was down, and his car phone was in view.

"Jeez, aren't you afraid to leave a car like this open?" she asked, looking for an alarm system to no avail.

"Anyone who would mess with my car would be sorry."

"Yeah, but anyone wouldn't know that up front, would he?" she asked, wondering exactly how sorry the miscreant might be.

She kept wondering as they took what Nick dubbed a sneak route that zigzagged behind the Strip. Maybe she was nuts to be giving Nick a shot. If he were a killer, one shot at her would be all he would need....

"So what have you heard?" Nick suddenly demanded.

Jarred from her thoughts, she asked, "About what, Nicky?"

"Don't play dumb."

Figuring he meant his family, Sasha cautiously said, "I heard your father did time."

"He did. What else?"

"That his connections got you the money for the Caribbean."

He neither confirmed nor denied that. "And?"

Did he expect her to bring up the murders? "Should there be more?" she asked instead.

"No. There shouldn't. But people speculate about lots of things they shouldn't. Human nature. They also don't think a leopard can change his spots. They're wrong."

Did he mean his father? Or himself?

He let her off the hook, and a few minutes later they arrived at the restaurant, one of the few fancy eateries on the Strip not connected with a big hotel-casino. The outside of *Donatelli's* was a study in good taste—no neon anywhere. The facade was of copper-glazed glass that glowed rich and elegant against the dusk.

The valet took over the car while Nick took over her, possessively sliding a hand around her waist. Sasha noticed but didn't let the fact get to her. Besides, she was too distracted by nerves over meeting his father.

The inside of the place was as classy as the outside, the walls that weren't glass were copper-tinted mirroring. The decor was elegant and understated, the seating a combination of copper tables, with either plush brown velvet booth benches or velvet chairs. And flowers everywhere.

They headed toward the inside of the restaurant, where a single booth was raised slightly and set off from the rest of the seating. Sasha figured this had been designed on purpose, to give status and an eagle's eye view to the restaurant's owner, who she assumed was the man already ensconced in the booth with a young woman. From the looks of her, she was no doubt Nick's sister. With surprise, Sasha recognized the dark-haired, green-eyed beauty as being the woman who'd been watching them from the slot machines the day before. Again she was wearing green.

And to the side of the owner's booth was a table with three men, all of whom looked like bodybuilders—or bodyguards. Vito Tolentino was one of them. He was watching *her.*

Sasha shook off the spooky feeling Vito gave her and concentrated on Nick's father, who stood graciously, then gave her a once over almost as thorough as had his son. "Nick, boy, you sure know how to pick 'em." He held out his hand to her. "Sally Donatelli."

Sasha shook. "Sasha Brozynski."

If she thought Salvatore Donatelli would look like some hardened type with scars or something, he wasn't. As a matter of fact, he looked very much like Nick—an older version with dark hair that was obviously a dye job, some wrinkles and a few extra pounds.

Sally released her hand. "And this is my daughter Caroline."

Who offered nothing more than an insincere smile and a, "How nice that you chose to join our *family* gathering."

Distressed by Caroline's rude tone, Sasha looked to the older Donatelli. "I hope I'm not intruding."

Nick's father was quick to say, "Not at all. It's a miracle my son finally has the sense to bring some beauty into my restaurant." He wagged a finger at his daughter. "Not that you aren't beautiful as well, Caroline."

"Thank you, Papa."

Nick helped her into the booth and Sasha found herself comfortably wedged between him and his father, with a subtly seething Caroline directly opposite.

But was Caroline angry with her or with Nick?

Sasha thought to diffuse the situation by dealing with the woman directly. "That's a stunning comb you're wearing," she said, admiring what had to be real diamonds and emeralds holding one side of her hair from her face.

"I bought her two, but I guess she prefers the Veronica Lake look," Sally told Sasha when Caroline didn't acknowledge the compliment. Then he said, "I hope you'll allow me to order for you."

Sasha smiled at him. "Of course."

"My father likes to give orders," Nick said loud enough for the older man to hear.

"And my son likes to ignore them."

While the two men were bantering, Sasha sensed a serious underlying tension that had to do with old business. Obviously Salvatore Donatelli had been unable to control his son for quite some time...if ever. For if she had ever met a man with a will of iron, Nick fit the bill.

"Apparently Nicky inherited more from his father than good looks," Sasha said to relieve any strain.

Sally laughed and Nick even smiled.

"*Nick* is in line to inherit more than personal traits from our father. Is that why you're interested?"

"Caroline—"

"No, Nick, let her answer."

Sasha looked Caroline straight in the eye and said, "I don't judge people by what they have or don't have . . . unless it's good manners."

Sally laughed again and threw an arm around Sasha's shoulders for a quick squeeze. "You have a woman who speaks her mind here. This one you should learn to appreciate."

"I already do," Nick said.

But the look Caroline gave her was pure poison.

For the next hour, Sasha ate her way through antipasto, stuffed artichoke hearts and linguini with roasted peppers and slivers of sausage. She was subtly aware of Vito keeping an eye on her even while Nick's father coaxed her into talking about her growing-up years in Ozone Park. Originally from Queens as well, Sally was familiar with the neighborhood, had even had a job once at Aqueduct Race Track. Thinking he didn't seem the type to groom horses, she wondered if that's where he got his start in crime, with some bookie working the track.

Not that she asked.

She found that she liked Nick's father—no matter his sordid past and possible present—though she couldn't say the same about his sister. Caroline held her tongue unless she aimed a shot at Sasha. Both men gave her warning looks, but Caroline was a true Donatelli and remained unintimidated.

Finally, declaring herself to be full, Sasha left the table, feeling Vito's gaze follow as she retired to the ladies' room to escape the continuing tension. She took her time. Washed her hands twice. Then sat in the outer room, intending to touch up her hair and makeup. But when she looked into the mirror, it was to see Caroline standing behind her.

"What's up?" Sasha asked, smoothing some stray hairs back into the slick style. "Couldn't get good enough zingers in with an audience?"

"I'm not going to pretend I like you for Nick's sake."

"I'd say you wouldn't like any woman Nicky brought to the table."

"His name is Nick. He hates being called Nicky."

"Not so I've noticed." Sasha swiped her lips with deep red lipstick.

Caroline fussed with the emerald-and-diamond comb. "You're only a temporary distraction, you know."

"Maybe I don't want to be anything more."

Still behind her, Nick's sister moved closer. "They all do. At first. And then they realize..." She didn't finish the dramatically begun statement.

"What? Who his father is. I already know."

"But there are so many things that you don't know." Caroline gave her a sly look. "And shouldn't know. You should get out while you can."

"Is that a threat?" Sasha demanded, whirling around on her stool. "Because if it's a threat, maybe I'll ask Nicky about it."

A smile hovered around Caroline's lips. "You do that."

Sasha rose. Even in flats she was taller than Nick's sister in heels. She felt like popping her one. But violence wasn't in her nature, and restraint was something her mother had taught her from childhood. So she smiled instead, and sauntered out of the rest room as if she weren't ticked off, as if Caroline's words were insignificant.

But she couldn't help wondering what Nick's sister meant.

Chapter Seven

"Sasha Brozynski, isn't it?"

Startled out of her reverie as she headed back to the table, Sasha looked up to see a silver-haired man bearing down on her. "Mr. VanDerZanden."

"Gaines," he said heartily, taking her hand and bringing it to his lips the way he had the night before. Then he turned her hand over and hovered over her wrist, inhaling. "Ah, even your scent is enchanting."

Noticing that, as he released her, his gaze wandered to her throat and stuck there, Sasha said, "And you're a born flatterer."

He didn't seem to hear. "Lovely pearls...almost as lovely as the lady." He seemed to be fixed on the jet clasp.

His intense focus on the choker made her squirm inside. "I borrowed them from a friend." Then she deliberately added, "JoJo Weston. Maybe you've seen them on her."

The blue eyes that met hers were frosty. "Maybe that's because I bought them for her."

Her hand moved to her throat. "You have excellent taste." Remembering Nick's comment about Gaines trying to buy JoJo away from him, she knew the pearls were real.

"How is JoJo?" he asked.

Was his tone really strange or was she imagining it?

"I wouldn't know." Watching him carefully, she said, "Seems she ran off to marry some mystery man."

He didn't even blink.

"Really. And what about you, Sasha? Have you decided whether or not you're attached?"

His now cool-sounding interest was making Sasha uneasy. She took comfort in being able to say, "I'm sure you know I'm here with Nicky."

"So it's Nicky, eh? I guess that answers my question...for the moment. I'm a man who doesn't give up easily when I want something."

He nodded and went on his way, leaving Sasha staring after him and wondering. Gaines VanDerZanden could be charming. And he was certainly good-looking. And as he said, he didn't give up easily.... But what was it that he wanted. *Her?* She doubted it. More likely, he was embroiled in a competition thing with Nick—first over JoJo, now her.

Was it possible that Gaines VanDerZanden could be JoJo's Hunkman?

Nick had denied Gaines might be the prospective groom, but what better way to get a girl's attention than to propose. He'd been off-balance about the pearls and had admitted he'd bought them for JoJo. Did a man give such an expensive present to a woman he wasn't serious about?

Not running in wealthy circles, Sasha wouldn't know. The question continued to bother her, though, as she made her way to rejoin the table. But, drawing closer, she realized all three Donatellis were in the midst of a serious discussion.

Sally tersely asked, "So, Nick, have you thought over my offer or not?"

His back to her, Nick growled in return. "This isn't the time to talk about it."

Realizing the discussion was more of an argument, Sasha chose not to approach the table. She stopped inches away from the bodyguards and gave Vito a nervous look.

"When would be a good time?" Sally was asking heatedly, his face growing ruddy. "You've been avoiding your responsibility. You owe the family—"

"I don't owe you this!"

"Nick," Caroline wheedled in a tone totally different from any Sasha had heard. "Papa only wants the best for all of his children."

"I know what's best for me. Why don't you put out a search warrant for Lucky and bring him home? See if you can force him to heel." Nick glanced around and caught Sasha listening. His expression was not pretty. "You ready to go?"

Startled by the unexpected hostility aimed her way, she said, "Anytime you are . . . Nicky."

His jaw tightened and he glared at her. "Then let's do it." Sliding out of the booth, he moved to leave immediately, but, pulse skittering, she skirted him and walked back to the table.

"Thank you for dinner," she told his father. "It was wonderful."

"My pleasure. You come back anytime as my guest," Sally said. "And don't wait for my son to bring you— a girl could starve to death first."

"You're a real gentleman," Sasha told him. Then she nodded at Nick's sister, merely saying, "Caroline."

When she looked for Nick, however, she realized he'd walked out on her. How rude. Thinking maybe she should get a taxi back to the apartment complex just to show him what she thought of his behavior, Sasha left the restaurant.

The Corvette was already parked at the entrance, engine running, Nick inside. Waiting for her impatiently, he was practically steaming.

She hesitated, trying to make up her mind.

"Get in!" he bellowed.

That did it.

She stalked away from him toward a parked taxi. Behind her, a growl and the sound of a car door being thrown open told her Nick wasn't letting her go so easily. She tensed and readied herself, expecting to be grabbed and spun around. But when she struck out at Nick, as she had the time he'd surprised her, he seized her wrist, effectively stopping her.

With a furious expression, he pulled her so close Sasha could feel his breath on her face when he said, "I told you that would only work once."

Heart thundering against her ribs, breath coming shallow and fast, she tried freeing her wrist to no avail. "You're hurting me!"

He wasn't really, but she figured her complaining would make him let go. It didn't. He dragged her back to the car. Fear sluiced through her. In his frame of mind, he could do anything. Alarms going off, Sasha told herself to fight him. She could get away if she really wanted to.

Or maybe die trying came a warning whisper in her head.

Problem was, she didn't know what she did or did not believe about Nick Donatelli . . . or what she did or did not want from him.

Before she could make up her mind, she was being held prisoner by a seat belt and Nick was driving as if the devil were perched on his rear bumper. Or at least on the foot that kept pressing the accelerator closer and closer to the floor. Flying down a side street, away from the glitz and glamour of the Strip, he was focused on nothing but speed.

And whether she liked it or not, Sasha was a captive participant . . . tempted to use his car phone to call for help.

Nails digging into the upholstery, she glanced over at him. He seemed unaware of her—and his anger seemed directed inward. She got the feeling that she'd merely been at the wrong place at the wrong time. That his father had been trying to control him somehow, and now Nick was proving that *he* was in control the easiest way possible. By bullying her.

Or maybe he just didn't like being rejected, that inner voice whispered.

She ignored what she didn't want to hear.

But when the Corvette barely missed another car going through an intersection, she cried, "For heaven's sake, Nicky, slow down before you get us both killed! Unless that's your intention."

Though Nick didn't bother to answer, she noticed the buildings stopped whizzing by at such an incredible pace. And his expression relaxed somewhat, his anger visibly dissipating as she watched. Adrenaline poured from her, leaving her drained, her limbs about as useful as putty. Taking a deep, calming breath, she leaned back against the seat and let him have a few minutes to chill out.

What was chewing at Nick's gut to make him so reckless? Had his father been demanding he do something illegal to pay back some favor? And if so, did that mean that, despite the rumors, Nick had refused because he walked the straight and narrow? And who the heck was Lucky, anyway?

Thinking she was fabricating—the family tug-of-war had probably been over something trivial—Sasha stared at Nick. And under the glow of passing streetlights, she could see that his expression was still closed, if not angry. Still, she was unable to contain her curiosity any longer.

"So what's got you so hot you're ready to burn out?" she demanded.

"It's personal."

"I thought we were getting personal." She echoed his own assertion that he'd used to get information from her about her attack.

Impatiently, he said, "This is family business."

In other words, it was none of hers. "I figured that part out." She persisted anyway. "Sometimes talking about your family helps. No one has a perfect situation one-hundred percent of the time. Disagreements are part of life."

"But I'm not obligated to give you explanations of any kind."

Which effectively put her in her place.

Sasha fumed the rest of the way home, making her realize that she had been putting more stock in this thing between her and Nick than just crazed hormones or some plan he'd seen through. What had she expected?

She'd been warned he went through show girls like peanuts.

That he might think she was just another tasty treat that he could help himself to before going on to the next one stirred all kinds of uncomfortable emotions in her. Emotions that scared her, told her she was out of control.

So when he pulled up to JoJo's complex and seemed about to find a parking spot—did he really imagine she'd want to be alone with him now?—she unclipped her seat belt and dashed a little cold water over his libido.

"You can let me out right here."

Nick came to a dead stop, and Sasha zipped out of the car and flounced down the walk as he called after her, "Look, I shouldn't have taken my bad temper out on you. " An apology that came too late to pacify Sasha. She didn't respond. Even before she reached the stairs, she heard the screech of tires and glanced back to see him burn rubber out of the complex.

"Good riddance," she muttered, half of her even meaning it.

The other half—the one that had no sense—brooded as she entered the apartment and kicked off her shoes. She slipped out of JoJo's dress and hung it back in the closet. What was wrong with her? Was she really falling for a man who might be a murderer? One who might be responsible for her friend's disappearance?

Removing the pearls reminded Sasha of Gaines VanDerZanden—made her wonder how long the man had been around...something she would try to find out at the first opportunity. She returned them to the jewelry case, wondering why JoJo hadn't secured them better.

And then it came to her. The simple wedding dress in JoJo's closet was decorated with pearls. What if she'd been planning to wear the choker for her wedding? And JoJo wasn't the type of woman who would wear jewelry from one man while marrying another. So, was it possible that Gaines VanDerZanden was the mysterious prospective bridegroom?

More confused than ever, she slammed the lid on the jewelry case and finished undressing. After a hot shower, she slid into a cotton nightshirt and climbed into bed, thinking she would be awake all night. But within minutes, her thoughts became muzzy and her breathing deepened ...

And then the telephone blasted her awake. Sasha sat up and turned on the nightstand lamp, trying to focus so she could find the phone.

Assuming Nick was calling to bug her, she lifted the receiver and said, ''This better be good!''

''Sasha?''

Her name was barely a sigh. A woman's voice. A strange woman calling her in the middle of the night. ''Yes?''

''...gotta help me.''

Sasha strained to decipher the woman's whispering. ''Who is this?'' Even trying hard, Sasha could barely make out the words.

''...crazy...won't let me go...''

And then it came to her. ''JoJo? My God, this is JoJo, isn't it?'' Before the caller could reply, the line went dead. ''JoJo!''

Shaking, Sasha stared at the receiver and went cold inside. If that had been her friend, who had stopped JoJo from completing the call? She hung up, willing the phone to ring again. But the only sound was her pulse rushing through her head.

JoJo . . . alive . . . thank God!

Once more she called the police, established that her friend had now been missing for two days, then went over the odd conversation—JoJo asking for help, saying someone was crazy, that the person wouldn't let her go.

"I think she was probably referring to the man she was supposed to have married."

"I need a name."

"I don't have one."

"Let's see what we have here," the cop on the other end said. "A call in the night. A whispered voice. And no details. This isn't exactly enough for us to go on."

Sasha realized she wasn't being taken seriously. "Look, my friend has been missing for your required forty-eight hours—"

"You're sure this was her? You recognized the voice?"

"Not exactly."

The cop sighed. "Well, we can look into it. . . ."

"You do that and let me know what you find out."

Sinking back against the pillows, Sasha figured her call had been a waste of time. Even so, she was elated to know JoJo was alive. And asking for Sasha's help must mean she was somewhere nearby. Maybe she could find her, after all.

She *would* find her, Sasha thought, determination renewed.

WHEN SASHA PULLED UP to the Gonna Get Married Chapel of Love the next afternoon, Reverend Floyd

Edelman was just finishing wedding vows for a middle-aged couple in a classic white convertible.

In the back seat of the newlyweds' car, "Elvis" played his guitar and sang "Falling in Love With You," as the groom started the ignition and pulled the vehicle from the lot, while the ponytailed bride rested her head on his shoulder. They were followed by two more convertibles—one powder blue, the other baby pink—holding the wedding party. All the aging participants were dressed in their sixties best. The minister had one foot inside the building before Sasha caught up with him.

"Excuse me, Reverend Edelman."

"May I help you?" He turned and looked at her as though he'd never seen her before.

"You remember me—Sasha Brozynski?"

"I'm afraid not." But his thready voice cracked on the lie.

She narrowed her gaze. "JoJo Weston's maid of honor?"

He shrugged and tried to escape.

Sasha grabbed the folds of his purple robes, stopping the slight man easily. "Not so fast, Rev."

"Young lady—"

"Either you talk to me or to the police."

Giving her an indignant expression, he said, "I have nothing to fear from the local constabulary."

"So, shall we call them together? We're talking about a missing person here. A felony."

The minister wilted before her eyes. "Let's go into my office."

He led her past a small lounge that was filled with wedding supplies available for purchase, then past a bride's room with mirrored walls. Finally they came to a small but luxuriously appointed office. Reverend Edelman closed the door behind her, and Sasha made herself comfortable in a leather chair.

His thready voice solemn, Reverend Edelman said, "You realize I am a man of God, and as such, am committed to a vow of silence where my flock is concerned."

Sasha gave him an exasperated look. "You're not a priest and you don't have a flock...unless you're talking about sheep. And I'm not asking you to reveal someone's confession here." She started. "Or am I?"

"No, no, nothing like that!" He sank into his chair.

"Then what? I'm not going away until you tell me, Rev, so you might as well fess up. Unless you want me to implicate you in the kidnapping, of course."

The minister caved in against his high-backed chair. "All right. But if anything happens to me for telling you..."

The implication being, it would be on her head. "Someone threatened you?"

He twitched and twittered and finally admitted, "In return for a generous amount of money, triple the full payment for the wedding...I was told it would be in my best interests to forget all about it."

"Someone wanted you to forget about the wedding that never happened? Who?"

"I'm afraid I don't know."

"C'mon. Stop playing games!" Sasha insisted. "My friend's in trouble."

"Yes, I realize that now."

Trying to figure out whether he was sincerely worried or merely trying to placate her to get her sympathy, she said, "So tell me."

"I'm telling you that I do not know. I received an envelope of cash with a typed note attached. No signature."

"So where is this note?"

"I threw it away, of course. I didn't want anyone to see it, to get the wrong impression."

"How ethical of you." Remembering JoJo's plea, that the person holding her wouldn't let her go, Sasha wondered again if she'd meant the man she'd planned on marrying. "Maybe the prospective groom sent the money."

"I have no idea. As I told you before, Miss Weston never even gave me his name."

"She didn't say anything about him?"

"Nothing. Well . . . only that she met him at the casino where she worked."

"Are you sure she didn't mean the showroom?"

"Positive. She said he'd helped her place a bet . . . and that it turned out to be the luckiest bet she'd ever made, because it brought them together."

"That's it? You don't have a clue as to his identity?"

"How could I? I never saw the marriage license."

Marriage license. Of course.

"And now, if you'll excuse me?" Reverend Edelman was saying.

Figuring she wasn't going to get more from the minister, Sasha rose. "You think of anything, you call me at the Island Showroom in the Caribbean. I'll make it worth your while," she added, appealing to his greed.

From the chapel, she headed straight for the city clerk's office. Marriage licenses were a matter of public record.

But half an hour later, her new bubble burst.

"Jane . . . Janet . . . Jennifer . . . Joyce . . . no JoJo Weston," the middle-aged clerk told her.

"You're sure? Can you check again? W-E-S-T-O-N."

The clerk typed onto the computer as Sasha spelled. She shook her head. "Sorry."

Frustrated yet again, Sasha headed her rental car toward the Caribbean—she'd actually be early for once. If JoJo really planned to have a wedding, why no license? Had she left that detail to the groom? If so, it seemed the man had never planned on marrying her friend. Damn it, who was he?

She thought about Edelman telling her the intended had helped JoJo place a bet. So far, Sasha had only been able to link her friend with three men—Nick Donatelli, Mac Schneider and Gaines VanDerZanden—any of whom could be the one, she realized. Though Mac hadn't claimed more than a passing friendship, with Barbie being the one he'd been dating. And who knew whether or not Gaines had gotten anywhere with her friend, despite the pearl choker?

Sasha swallowed the lump that stuck in her throat at the notion of Nick's possibly being the guilty one. Even after the way he'd treated her the night before, she knew she had feelings other than anger for Nick Donatelli.

What a situation. Here for six months she'd been avoiding men like the plague...and now the plague had found her. Sasha only hoped it wouldn't kill her. A chill shot up her spine at the thought that she might already have put herself in mortal danger. Well, she couldn't stop now. Hearing from JoJo had renewed her sense of purpose.

Traversing the casino to the showroom, she couldn't help looking for Nick, couldn't help the disappointment when she didn't find him. And the people who were gaming reminded her of Reverend Edelman's story about how JoJo met her fiancé... about how JoJo's intended had helped her place some kind of a bet.

"Hey, why so serious?"

Sasha's heart raced as Mac surprised her by appearing out of nowhere. Because he was wearing his dealer's vest, she asked, "Are you on the job?" Then wondered if that bet hadn't been at Mac's blackjack table.

"Not till five. How about we share another cup of coffee? Dinner, even."

Though her stomach growled at the suggestion, she said, "No, but thanks."

Mac checked his watch. "You've got nearly two hours till show time."

"There's going to be an early run-through with the whole company in about half an hour," Sasha told him. "Besides, I never eat before a show. Too nervous." Half the truth. If she didn't want to avoid his company for the moment, she could have something small this early.

"After, then?" he persisted.

"I had a late night. I'll be ready to sack out while you're still working."

"I can get off early."

"How about a rain check?"

Though he appeared decidedly unhappy about the brush-off, Mac forced a smile. "Sure. A rain check."

She left him standing there in her wake, feeling his eyes on her back, a sense of unease inching up her spine. Why was he so darn insistent on getting to know her better?

Because of JoJo?

Wondering if she could figure out which locker belonged to her friend, Sasha decided to ransack it for information, something she hadn't had the opportunity to do, yet.

But, upon arriving at the dressing room, her purpose was put on hold. Neatly leaning against the front of her locker was an eight-by-ten envelope. Her name was printed across the front in black marker, and she thought the handwriting was familiar.

She sat in front of the makeup mirrors and opened the envelope. The contents were familiar, too. Copies of newspaper articles detailing the deaths of Mia Scudella and Glory Hale. Who had left this for her? And why? To warn her off of seeing Nick? Did someone send a like package to any woman he was interested in?

Sasha had already read the contents of JoJo's copies several times. In an attempt at making sense of what someone was trying to tell her, she took a closer look at the stuff in her hands, comparing the two crimes. The murders had been committed in the same way. She knew that. But the women were very different.

Glory Hale had been from a small farming community in Nebraska. She'd grown up poor and had been the middle child of seven. The job as a Las Vegas show girl had been her break into the big time.

Mia Scudella, on the other hand, had been born and raised in Las Vegas with only one sibling; her twin brother, Marco. She came from money. And not just any money. *Laundered money.* Her father, Carmine, had been a *business* associate of Sally Donatelli.

Before she could make anything of the information that she suspected had to mean something, voices warned her others were arriving. Quickly she stuffed the copies back into the envelope, then secreted the packet in her locker.

And turned to find Nick leaning against the door-jamb, staring.

Chapter Eight

Had he seen the envelope? The contents?

Nick's gaze was intent on *her,* making Sasha wonder if he knew what she was hiding. He also seemed wary—but what did he have to be cautious about?

Despite her good sense, despite the rough way he'd treated her the night before, Sasha felt heat rise through her body. Furious with herself, she crossed her arms protectively over her chest, choosing to give him the hard time he so richly deserved.

"You must be lost, Nicky," she said sweetly. "This is the women's locker room."

"I'm exactly where I meant to be. The surprise is that you are, too," he said, and she imagined something like relief colored the words. "I thought you might take a powder on me after last night."

"Why?" Purposely she drew closer, eyes wide. "Am I supposed to be afraid of you?"

His expression became serious and he told her, "Some would say so."

"What do you say?"

"I say...I can't get you out of my head."

Nick stepped away from the door, closer to her. Sasha damned the pounding of her heart, tried convincing herself it was due to a dose of healthy fear rather than attraction.

Though he seemed about to walk through her, she stood her ground and demanded, "Try harder!"

"Impossible."

Stopping with millimeters to spare, he reached out and ran a single finger up along her arm. Goose bumps followed. His gaze caught hers, and in the depths of his green eyes she read hot desire. Her breasts tightened and a knot of sexual tension gathered deep in her belly. Her breath caught in her throat, and she found herself swaying toward him....

In a desperate attempt to regain her equilibrium, Sasha spun around and moved away from Nick, giving herself some safe space. "I didn't appreciate your manhandling me last night, Nicky." Even as she remembered, her blood was racing, thrumming in her ears. Was she actually attracted to danger? "I'm not looking forward to a repeat performance."

"What if I tell you there won't be one?"

"Why should I believe you?"

"My mood had nothing to do with you."

"Nah, you only took it out on me."

"A mistake," he admitted. "My apologies. Can't we pick up where we left off?"

"We didn't leave off any place good."

"Then let's back up a few steps—to before dinner."

Mightily tempted, Sasha forced herself to think of JoJo's cry in the night... added to the stories of Nick's women who hadn't survived their relationships with him. Or rather, their rejections. She'd plotted to repeat their performances—to reel him in, then to reject him and see where it took her. His insight into her half-baked plot had made her give that up...and yet, hadn't she rejected Nick in a small way the night before?

Just her turning her back on him had made his temper flare.

Any relationship between them would be complicated, and even if she hadn't withstood an attack, she wouldn't put up with being handled roughly by any man. Then again, Nick hadn't actually tried to hurt her, merely to impose his will on her.

"We have something special, you and I," Nick was murmuring.

He was trying to impose his will now. He was using physical force without touching her. His very powerful presence was so effective that Sasha found herself backed into a corner. Figuratively and literally. She found herself pressed against the lockers, Nick's hands flattened on either side of her head. He was leaning toward her...threatening her...then carrying through with the sensual threat by kissing her.

She certainly couldn't stop him. And she couldn't help herself, either. Her bones were putty in his hands. Worse, her brain was mush. Instinct made her kiss him back.

For one moment, Sasha was lost. She wrapped her arms around his neck and savored a passion she hadn't known she was capable of. Her only focus was Nick, as his mouth conquered hers. Thoroughly. His experienced tongue sliding inside, insinuating itself as if it belonged there. He took her very breath away and left her wanting more. Especially when he broke the slow deep kiss that had held her enthralled. She whispered a protest, but he nuzzled it away.

His teeth nipped first at her lower lip, then went for the soft, responsive flesh between her neck and shoulder. Her eyes fluttered closed, and the pulse sped up in her throat. Her breath shallow and quick, Sasha arched her neck and slid against the locker, the handle jamming her in the hip, the metal suddenly cold against the exposed skin of her back.

Providing her with a reality check.

Through a haze of desire, she remembered the documents inside her locker. Remembered that Nick might be a murderer, might be holding her friend hostage...

"Don't let me interrupt anything."

Barbie's irritated and irritating voice was as effective as a splash of cold water. Sasha's eyes flashed open to see the blonde staring at them in disgust. Realizing they had even more of an audience—several show girls had entered the dressing room and were rubbernecking to get a good look—Sasha was pushing at Nick's chest.

But Nick wasn't budging. He was ignoring everything but her. "So what do you say, gorgeous?"

She blinked into his smug expression. He expected her to cave in, to agree to see him. He was using his sexuality to conquer her. And she was tempted to let him. Only she had more pride than that. More sense. More of a liking for her own skin. How could she trust him?

Having no answer, Sasha swallowed hard and said, "Take a hike, Nicky," soft enough so that no one else in the room would hear.

His eyes immediately hardening to emeralds, he backed off, displeasure written on his drop-dead gorgeous face for a moment before he changed, chameleonlike. In a heartbeat, he became aloof, mocking, unreachable. While his armor was up, his gaze bored into hers as if he were taking a walk inside her head.

Seeming satisfied, he nodded and left the dressing room without another word.

And Sasha felt as if a piece of her left with him.

"Not satisfied with the rumba?" Barbie sniped, as if forgetting she was supposed to be friendly. She dumped her bag on the makeup counter and sat before the mirror. "Play your cards right and maybe you can convince Mr. D to have Yale create a solo expressly for you."

And Sasha suddenly realized exactly how resentful the blonde could be of someone who might be getting further than she was. Had she been jealous of JoJo? For a moment, she saw Barbie in a different light . . . as someone who might do anything to rid herself of a rival. Then she realized how silly that sounded. JoJo had disappeared because of a man.

"I don't use people to get ahead," she told Barbie, as other dancers opened their lockers and started getting ready for the preshow run-through.

"Could have fooled me."

"Look, I'm not trying to take anything from anyone here. I'm just trying to survive."

"Well, you're doing a spectacular job of it, honey," the blonde said, turning her full attention on her mirror image. "Just think of how much damage you could do to the rest of us if you really tried."

If only Barbie knew the truth. The way things were going, the damage would be to Sasha—if not physically, then to her heart. Her emotions were too wrapped up with Nick Donatelli for her own peace of mind.

LESTER PERKINS patiently waited in the shadows of the hallway outside the dressing rooms. Seemed that was all he ever did. Waited for something to happen to him.

Mr. D knew how to make things happen. Like with Sasha Brozynski. Lester figured she was going to be Mr. D's new woman if nothing stopped it . . . even if he *had* heard them arguing and Mr. D had stormed out of the dressing room looking mad enough to kill.

He could go for Sasha, too, Lester thought. She was nice, maybe as nice as JoJo. If he tried real hard, maybe he could convince her that he was nice, too.

Show girls were leaving the dressing room in their glitzy costumes that left little to the imagination. He'd always had a good one. He could imagine himself with Sasha, for example, just like he had with JoJo. But imagining wasn't as satisfying as the real thing. He knew that now. He'd stopped hiding in the shadows, waiting for his turn. He'd learned to be bold, to make things happen.

So when Sasha stepped out of the dressing room, he approached her. "Your first night. Good luck . . . I mean break a leg, right?"

She smiled. *At him.*

"Thanks, Lester. I appreciate the kind words."

She appreciated him!

He punched at his glasses, smearing a lens in his excitement. "Maybe we could celebrate, after? Go have a drink in the Coral Reef Bar?"

"That's sweet of you to offer, but tonight's not a good night."

She thought he was sweet. And she was willing to see him another night!

Lester smiled. "All right, then. Another time."

Her smile faded a bit. "Um, I don't think so, Lester. But thank you very much for offering."

With that, she hurried for the backstage door. And Lester stood there, filled with anger and fighting tears. She'd led him on. Made him believe she was the one.

Who did she think she was, turning *them* down?

AFTER THE LATE SHOW, Yale Riker knocked at the dressing room door and entered before anyone told him he could. Luckily, the few girls who hadn't left were all dressed, not that he seemed concerned.

"Flowers for our newest show girl," he said dramatically, waving a cut-crystal vase full of roses.

Sasha's heart thrummed as she moved to claim the roses. From Nick? Maybe she'd been too hard on him. She nuzzled a blossom and sniffed.

"Mmm, how beautiful," she murmured.

Yale shoved the crystal vase into her hands. "He said to tell you, 'they're nearly as beautiful as you'."

"Nicky said that?"

"Heavens, no. Gaines VanDerZanden. He asked me to ask you if you would like to get a late dinner with him."

Hiding her disappointment, Sasha said, "Would you be a doll and make my excuses? I need sleep more than I need food." Not exactly a lie. She was emotionally exhausted. "But tell him I appreciate the offer and love the flowers."

"Will do," Yale said, spinning on his heel. "Though I'll be breaking the poor man's heart."

Would he? Or was Gaines trying to buy her away from Nick—as he had tried to do with JoJo—out of some bizarre sense of competition? How curious, considering Gaines probably attracted his share of bright, attractive women. Curious, too, that all three of her suspects had approached her tonight—first Mac, then Nick, now Gaines.

And Lester Perkins, a little voice added. What had that been all about? She'd barely spoken to the maintenance man before. Then she remembered Nick saying Lester was a poor bastard who mooned over show girls rather than finding a woman who would appreciate him.

Several more dancers left for the night, leaving only Barbie and Sasha in the dressing room. As usual, Sasha was running late. She'd taken an extra long shower to loosen the knots of tension tightening her back and neck, which had more to do with Nick than an opening night. She set the flowers on the makeup counter and hurriedly gathered her things.

"I'm really sorry about our tiff earlier," Barbie told her. "I'd like us to be friends."

"I'm glad," Sasha said truthfully. She didn't need tension from a co-worker. She was creating enough for herself to last a lifetime. Remembering the photo of JoJo and Barbie and Mac, she said, "You and JoJo are friends, right?"

Barbie hesitated only a second before echoing, "Right," but it was long enough for Sasha to wonder.

And long enough for her to improvise. "I'm sure JoJo mentioned doing some fun activity with you and Mac recently."

"She and Mac asked me to come along on a drive through red rock country."

That information startled Sasha, for Barbie made it sound like JoJo had been the one dating Mac, contrary to what he'd told her. Which was it?

"I got the impression you and Mac were a casual couple."

A sly smile hovered around Barbie's mouth as she said, "Mac's not my type." She gathered her makeup bag. "Well, this was a great opening night for you. You deserved the rumba," she added a bit too sincerely. "And the flowers. So, want to walk out to the parking lot together?"

"Thanks, Barbie, but I have to search the stage for one of my earrings. I lost it during the last number. Uh, you wouldn't want to stick around until I do, would you?"

"Leave it. Lester will find it when he's cleaning up."

"I think I'll look myself, anyway." Then Sasha asked, "Say, you wouldn't know which locker was JoJo's?" She still meant to search it.

"Somewhere in the middle of that second row." Barbie shouldered her bag and left Sasha alone.

Thinking she'd get back to the locker after finding the earring, a very expensive shoulder duster of crystals, Sasha set about her quest. Backstage, she grabbed a flashlight she'd spotted earlier and made her way into the showroom. Both stage and house lights were off. She clicked on the flashlight and ran the beam over the stage apron as she started her search.

Uneasily, she concentrated on her task, trying not to think about being the straggler again. She was tired of being afraid, of restructuring every facet of her life because of one incident in the past. She'd worked at getting over it for months. She wasn't about to regress now.

Certain the creepy feeling suddenly trailing her could be attributed to those bad memories, she focused her energies on finding that earring, an expensive item to replace. Foot by foot she thoroughly covered the apron and ramp that jutted into the audience. Then she wondered if perhaps she could have lost it when the stage elevator—a whole section of the floor—had taken the show girls down to one of the lower levels that housed sets and props.

Thinking she heard the whisper of footsteps nearby, Sasha went still. She clenched inside and settled her mind by running the flashlight on the area surrounding her. Nothing. Rather, nothing but nerves, Sasha assured herself.

When the stage floor gave up no sparkle, she approached the arched stairway that flattened into a walkway behind the twenty-thousand-gallon tank of water for the synchronized swimmers. The finale had started and ended on the stairway with show girls costumed as crystal-bedecked treasures from the deep—seashells and sand dollars, starfish and octopi—and, being the tallest of the show girls, she had been stationed on the walkway in the very middle. As she ascended, she checked each stair carefully, running the flashlight beam from one side to the other.

Halfway up the steps, she stopped, the hairs on the back of her neck prickling. The feeling that someone else was out there, watching her from the dark, was too strong to ignore.

"Hello? Is someone there?" she called, again sweeping the flashlight around her.

No answer.

Her pulse began to thrum as the beam washed the surrounding area, falling short of the apron's edge. Anyone could be in the audience and she would never know for certain.

So what should she do?

She considered for a moment, then chose to continue scanning the arch for her earring. She could be wrong about someone being there, but she would remain on her guard. Very definitely on her guard.

Heart thumping in an odd rhythm, she went on. Only upon reaching the bridge that ran behind the tank did she see a familiar sparkle.

She stilled the flashlight beam for a better look. There it was, the expensive piece of jewelry, caught in the crack between the two platforms that made up the walkway connecting the arched stairs. Still uncomfortable, swearing she sensed another presence nearby, Sasha carefully stooped to free the earring. Wedged tight in the crack, it wouldn't budge.

"Damn!" she cursed softly.

Taking a nervous look around, she dropped to one knee for a better view as well as some leverage. The earring dangled over the tank of water, stopped only by a single strand of crystals. If she didn't manipulate the strand carefully, she would ruin the earring.

Thinking to work quickly and get the hell out of there, she set the flashlight down next to her knee, the beam directed onto the crystals that shone like fire. She had to lean forward, over the water tank, to get one hand under the platform. She grasped the crystal strand from below with one hand, above with the other. After a few moments of cautious handling, she was able to free the earring.

Even as she was taking a breath of relief, she heard a sound behind her. Crystals grasped tight in one hand, she quickly picked up the flashlight with the other so she could see who stalked her.

Not fast enough.

For even as she was turning, the beam aiming for the intruder, a threatening shadow was upon her. Literally. She barely saw a dark silhouette before a hard shove sent her flying sideways off the platform. She tried to catch herself—letting go of both earring and flashlight—but her balance was precarious, and she couldn't get a grip on the walk.

Her stomach dropping faster than the rest of her, her leg bouncing hard off the safety glass, she fell directly into the drink with a huge splash and plunged straight to the bottom of the tank. Holding her breath, she struggled to get her feet under her and then bounced upward. When she broke surface, she was gasping and swallowing water.

The flashlight floated barely a yard away.

Coughing, she managed to yell, "Who the hell are you, you coward?"

A soft, sexless laugh was her only answer.

Sasha grabbed the flashlight—luckily it was waterproof—but washed the walkway and stairs with its pale beam too late. Her attacker had disappeared like a phantom into the cavernous backstage area.

Now to get herself out.

She stared up and immediately realized why ropes were lowered to lift the synchronized swimmers out of the pool of water—the ropes or a portable ladder were the only way anyone could get out easily. Even with her superior reach, her fingers didn't come near the top of the tank.

She told herself to remain calm. She was a good swimmer. She'd always loved the water. She wasn't going to drown. She had only to figure out a way to launch herself high enough to hook a hand over the top.

Which Sasha soon learned was definitely harder than she'd imagined.

For no matter how powerfully she lunged herself upward from the bottom, her fingers never quite reached the ledge. She tried launching herself from one side of the tank to the other. Even less effective.

Out of breath and with exhaustion setting in fast, she tried not to panic. But what was she to do? She came to terms with the impossibility of getting out by herself. That meant she had to attract someone's attention. But whose? Everyone was gone.

Everyone but the person who'd shoved her into the tank.

And maybe the maintenance man....

Hoping Lester Perkins and the culprit weren't one and the same, hoping that he was nearby as he always seemed to be, she yelled at the top of her already tiring lungs.

"Help! Someone help me! I'm in the swimmer's tank!"

Sasha waited a moment. Then yelled again. Wait. Yell. Wait. Yell. She didn't know how much time passed before she realized she didn't have the energy to try again.

The truth dawned on her. She would have to wait until someone returned to the theater, possibly until the next evening. But could she do it? Could she keep herself awake long enough to be rescued?

To save energy, Sasha went very still, her legs barely flexing, just enough to keep her upright. She leaned her head back, rested it against the water. Allowed her body to float up horizontally. Allowed the water to cradle her, calm her. Was tempted to close her eyes.

Floating, she searched for the flashlight. The beam glowed from the other end of the tank, making her feel not entirely alone. The light had bobbed far out of her reach. How long would the batteries last? How long before she would be thrown into utter darkness?

Without light, sleep would claim her, and if she fell asleep, Sasha knew she would drown. So she had to stay awake. Had to keep her mind working....

She replayed JoJo's cry for help, went over the people she had met in the last couple of days, the suspicions they'd raised for her. She was so busy forcing herself to think so as not to sleep, that she almost missed it.

A voice muffled by the water around her ears.

"Sasha?"

She couldn't recognize the voice but could tell it came from backstage.

Instinct taking over, she let her bottom sink and screamed, "Here! In the tank! Help me, please!"

Leather slapped wood as her rescuer closed the distance between them. She twirled around with a whoosh of water to see legs ascending the steps. But whose?

"Sasha? My God, how did you get in there? Are you all right?"

Heart thundering in her chest, she looked up into the shadowed expression of Nick Donatelli.

Chapter Nine

"How the hell did you get in there?" Nick demanded.

Tempted to ask him why the hell he'd been looking for her after everyone else had left—not to mention whether or not he'd had anything to do with her fall— Sasha held her tongue. An accusation would only put Nick off when she needed his help. Besides, if Nick had been the one to push her in, why would he have come back to help her out of the pool?

"Get me out of here," she said, "and then we'll talk."

"Right."

But rather than leaving to turn on the lights and fetch a ladder or find the switch that would lower the ropes, Nick merely leaned over and offered her his hand. Sasha hesitated only a moment before reaching for him. When she did, his fingers closed firmly around her wrist.

"I'm afraid I don't have much energy left," she gasped, "so you'll be doing most of the work here."

"Piece of cake. When I get you up high enough, grasp the ledge with your free hand."

He didn't wait for her to agree, merely hoisted himself upright and her with him. Finding the ledge was easy. Sasha only hoped she could hold on. But Nick didn't keep her dangling. With his free hand, he reached down and grabbed the waistband of her pants.

"Ready..."

Grunting, he hauled her upward and Sasha scrambled, grasping the walkway and shooting forward so that her chest rested on the flat surface. Drained of energy, she lay there, half on, half off the thing, feeling as if she might never be able to move again. Then Nick hooked an arm around her waist, another around her thigh, and towed her the rest of the way.

Somehow, Sasha found herself lying against him and cradled in his arms, with no desire to move. Her heart was beating hard, and not only from the exertion. Nick had saved her from a miserable unknown number of hours...maybe even from death.

But she was safe now.

"You don't mind if I stay here a moment, just until I catch my breath?"

Voice gruff, he said, "Stay as long as you like."

That might be forever. "You don't mind that I'm getting you all wet?"

"I'll dry out. You should have told me you wanted to take a swim. I would have opened the pool for you."

"Ha-ha." She couldn't even summon a real chuckle to reward his attempt at humor.

"So give."

Knowing Nick wouldn't let her off the hook until he was satisfied with a complete explanation, she began, "I was looking for the earring that I lost in the finale." Realizing she didn't have it in her hand, she tried to sit up. "Omigod, the earring's in the tank." Not that she could see it through the glow of the still-floating flashlight. "It probably sank straight to the bottom."

He pulled her back against his chest. "Don't even think about going back in there to get it."

"Trust me, I wasn't."

"So you were looking for the earring and..."

Assuring herself again that Nick wasn't the culprit, Sasha said, "Then I spotted the crystals stuck between platforms up here. And while I was trying to free it—"

"You fell in."

"More like I was pushed," she admitted. "I, uh, had this creepy feeling I wasn't alone right from the first. I guess my instincts were right on."

"So why didn't you leave the stage?"

"I called out and ran the flashlight around me, but I didn't see anyone," she argued. "I thought maybe my imagination was running overtime."

"Like when you thought someone followed you home last night?"

"Yeah, like then."

Sasha swallowed hard and waited for Nick's reaction. She felt the tightening of his muscles, but he didn't comment. Instead, he started to rise, lifting her with him.

"C'mon, you need to dry off."

Sasha stood unsteadily, and it took her a moment to realize why one leg seemed shorter than the other. "Great. I lost a shoe in there, too."

"I'll have someone fetch it and the earring."

Certain the leather would already be ruined by the water, she removed the second shoe, thinking she might as well throw it away and go home barefooted.

The air-conditioning against her wet skin made her shiver all the way to the dressing room, where she started to gather her things from her locker. Deciding she didn't really want to walk through the hotel-casino in bare feet—bad enough that she looked like a drowned rat—she slipped on a pair of dance shoes.

Watching her every movement, Nick asked, "Don't you think you should take a hot shower?"

Which she could do right there...if the thought didn't give goose bumps to her goose bumps. "I really want to get out of here. I can be home in twenty minutes."

"You can be at my place in five."

About to argue the point, Sasha changed her mind. With someone so obviously after her, she didn't relish being alone. At least not until she felt a little better. Shock was setting in and she was starting to shake inside as well as out.

But before she agreed, she needed some assurances. "What were you doing looking for me, anyhow?"

From his instant scowl, she could tell he knew exactly what was bothering her.

"I was hoping maybe I could change your mind about giving us another chance, so I waited outside for you. When people stopped coming out of the showroom, I first figured you were late as usual. Eventually, I started wondering and came inside to find out for myself."

That sounded plausible. Hoping she wasn't a fool, Sasha chose to believe Nick's explanation. "Maybe I can find a costume or something to put on after that shower," she said, barely keeping her teeth from chattering.

"Don't worry about it."

She shouldered her bag. "You have a supply of women's clothing in your apartment?" Not that the fact should surprise her.

"I was thinking more of a thick terry robe...while your clothes are in the dryer."

Imagining his robe next to her skin warmed her from the inside out. She nodded her agreement and left the dressing room with Nick, hoping that she wouldn't present too much of a spectacle on the way to the elevator.

Probably because Las Vegas was filled with odd sights, not more than a handful of people seemed to notice her unusual appearance. And thankfully, she and Nick took the ride up without other spectators.

Once inside his apartment, he led her into a stunning bedroom with red lacquered walls and black lacquered furniture. The floors were a natural wood, scattered with Oriental area rugs of the same colors. From the personal articles on the chest and nightstand, Sasha knew this was Nick's own bedroom rather than a guest room.

He opened the door to the bath and indicated she should enter. "Throw your clothes out here and I'll get them into the dryer and make you some hot tea. You'll find a linen closet with plenty of fresh towels and a couple clean robes to choose from."

Passing by him, she stopped a moment to share her gratitude. "Thanks for fishing me out, Nick."

He leaned close enough so she could feel his breath on her face. "Nick?"

Caught by the possessive gleam in his gorgeous green eyes, Sasha instinctively knew he wanted her to say, "Nicky."

His serious expression softened. "Now hurry, before you catch your death."

She slid by him, her goose bumps protesting. With the door closed, she peeled out of her wet clothes, then gathered them up, hesitating only when she got to her underwear. Though why she should be embarrassed at the thought of Nick handling her lacy underthings, she had no idea. Nick Donatelli had probably seen plenty of women's lingerie.

"Here you go." She cracked the door open and slid her hand out long enough to let him take the garments from her, then retreated.

His "Take your time" was a bit muffled by the sound of the lock popping in place.

Not that she didn't trust him....

The bath matched the bedroom. Red walls, black fixtures. The Jacuzzi for two, parked at the window overlooking the Strip, set her imagination going, but she tried to ignore the fantasy that conjured up, this being Nick's own bathroom. From the closet, she chose black towels and a red robe and hung them on hooks outside the shower stall.

The pulsating hot water felt good, warmed her from the inside out, and lifted a bit of the exhaustion from her shoulders. Even so, she was too tired to figure out who had pushed her into the tank. Having had enough water for one day, Sasha didn't care to linger.

Wrapping a towel around her wet hair turban-style, she quickly dried off and climbed into Nick's robe. The plush terry hung just above her ankles and wrapped almost twice around her middle. She even had to roll up the sleeves. She'd worn a man's robe more than once in the past, but never one that made her feel so...feminine.

The sneeze that followed countered that thought. She grabbed a tissue and went in search of Nick. She wandered through the living area and found him in a sleek, white-tiled kitchen. His back to her, he was preparing a tray. From the stove, a teakettle whistled, and over in the corner, a dryer hummed, ostensibly with her clothes.

She sneezed again.

He whipped around and studied her for a moment. Unable to tell if he liked what he saw, she self-consciously shifted from one foot to the other.

"Anything I can do?"

"You can pick the kind of tea you like," he said, going for the kettle.

On the island sat a basket filled with aromatic packets. She chose a soothing almond flavor and placed the bag in the china pot. He poured the boiling water, then, picking up the tray, led the way into the living room.

Curled up in one corner of the sofa with her mug, Nick sitting barely a yard away, she said, "I never would have thought you were so domestic."

"Making tea doesn't exactly qualify me for the Betty Crocker award," he said dryly.

"I don't know. You looked pretty much at home in the kitchen."

"Self-defense. I learned my away around a kitchen so I wouldn't have to eat all my meals in a restaurant. It doesn't mean I'm good at it."

Thinking about the family restaurant, she said, "What about *Donatelli's*—ever work there?"

"*Donatelli's* hasn't been around that long. My father had it built the last year he was incarcerated. Part of his plan to start a new life."

A life without crime? Sasha wondered. Remembering how hot he'd gotten over his father's mysterious request the night before, she pushed anyway. "So the restaurant is Sally's only business now?"

Nick wore a poker face when he said, "He has some other interests."

"Like . . . ?"

"Laundromats and food suppliers."

"No hotel-casino interests?" she asked, wondering about the Caribbean itself.

"That would not be looked upon favorably by the Feds."

She noticed he hadn't said *no,* however.

"So, who kept your father's interests floating while he was away?"

"Does it matter?"

"You tell me," she said, wiping at her nose with the tissue. The long soak in the tank was getting to her.

"In the beginning, some associates of my father's—with Vito's help, of course."

Vito. Nick's alibi for both of the murders. Trying not to think of them, wanting to believe in Nick's complete innocence, she said, "Growing up without a father must have been rough."

"I ran wild," he admitted, "especially after Mama died. I organized floating craps games in high school. I was in my senior year and about to be expelled when Vito took me in hand, threatened me within an inch of my life if I didn't get it together. He pushed me to get through school...all the way through Harvard Business School at that."

"Is that when you took over your father's affairs?" Sasha guessed.

Nick gave her a look that made her think he wouldn't answer, but in the end he said, "Me and Lucky."

"Lucky?"

"My younger brother, Lucian. He insisted on quitting school. Then Caroline came on board after getting her degree in business."

And Sasha had the distinct impression that Caroline itched to run the family corporation. "So what is Lucky doing now?"

"Your guess is as good as mine. Before our father was released from prison, Lucky took a powder on us all."

She couldn't miss the bitterness in his voice. "And you chose to open the Caribbean rather than work for your father."

"A man needs something of his own to build."

Something legitimate? Another sneeze prevented her from asking.

Nick studied Sasha with concern. She was too pale—except for her red nose—and her eyes were a little cloudy, like she might have a fever. "Hey, how are you feeling?"

"Not too terrific," she admitted, rubbing her arms briskly. "Maybe you can lower the air-conditioning?"

But the apartment wasn't cold. "The air's on low. You're chilled. Maybe I should call a doctor."

"No doctor! I've had enough doctors for a lifetime," she grumbled.

"Then let *me* play doctor," Nick suggested, thinking she would be all right as long as she kept warm. "I'll get something to heat you up inside."

"Not more mescal."

Remembering her reaction to the stuff last time, he smothered a grin. "I was thinking of brandy."

While he was getting the bottle and glasses, Sasha curled up into a ball on the couch. She looked uncommonly vulnerable. Vulnerable enough to tell him what he wanted to know? She'd gotten more out of him than he liked, though there were a lot more incriminating questions she could have asked. And he would have avoided answering.

Nick waited until he had a jigger of booze in her before he started probing. "So what made you decide to be a dancer?'' Start with something easy in order to put her off guard.

"My mom. She was in love with old movies, especially anything with Fred and Ginger. She danced around the house a lot, especially when she was cleaning. Her escape, I guess. Anyway, I was maybe five when she asked me if I wanted to take dance lessons. I said yes and my fate was set.''

"So your mother approves of what you do?'' he asked, splashing a bit more brandy into her glass.

"Sure. Why wouldn't she? Both my parents do. My dad couldn't be more proud.''

She punctuated the statement with another sneeze.

"Still cold?''

"No, just feeling a little woozy.''

"Let the doctor take over.'' He pulled Sasha against him and wrapped an arm around her. Her legs were stretched half the length of the couch, and she wedged her bare feet under a cushion. When he was certain she was comfortable, if not totally relaxed, he said, "It's good that you work at something you love.''

"I'm lucky.''

"And talented.'' He paused a moment, then went for the jugular. "So why did you stop dancing last fall?''

She twisted around to look at him. Her expression was guarded. "I already told you.''

"I know. You were mugged or *something*. Bad enough so you couldn't work for six months?''

She looked away and wet her lips. "Yes.''

"Broken bones?''

Hesitating a moment, she added, "And a broken spirit.''

Certain the brandy had the power to loosen her tongue, he rubbed her arm through the terry robe and insisted, "Tell me."

She heaved a sigh. "I was attacked backstage after a show."

"Someone broke into the theater?" When she seemed reluctant to tell him more, he urged, "C'mon, you can't stop now. It might do you some good to talk about it. Besides, I'll be after you until you spill your guts."

She trembled against him and he tightened his hold. He was feeling protective . . . even if he was determined to reveal all of Sasha's secrets.

She began, "This guy was a former football player, and a former boyfriend of another dancer. Dave Haskell," she added, naming a famous quarterback. "He'd had too much to drink, and then bribed the security guard to let him in during the show. Leslie wasn't too thrilled to see him, I can tell you. She sent him on his way. Or so she thought. Haskell waited for her backstage, but somehow he missed her. I was the last one to leave, as usual . . . so he took it out on me."

Realizing how difficult this was for her, Nick pressed his arm around her encouragingly and kept his tone even. "He took it out how?"

"He came on to me, saying one dancer was as good as another. I didn't want to offend him—he was drunk and I figured broken-hearted—so I tried putting him off nicely."

"And he wouldn't take no for an answer, right?"

"He got rough, but I wasn't what you would call a docile victim. I screamed. I scratched and kicked. Only thing was, he kicked back and worse." He felt her shudder as she said, "Before the security guard came to my rescue, Haskell had managed to break a couple of my ribs, dislocate my left shoulder, and bloody up my face.''

Now knowing why she'd resorted to using self-defense techniques on him when he'd frightened her, Nick swore under his breath and held her tighter. ''I hope the bastard is in jail where he belongs.''

She tensed, saying, ''Fat chance.''

''You're not going to tell me you didn't even try.''

''Oh, I had him arrested. Then Haskell claimed I came on to him because he was famous. He said I started to scream and maul him when he wasn't interested. He swore he was only defending himself.''

Nick was stunned. ''The police bought that?''

''I'm not sure what they bought—I'm not exactly your average-size woman. Anyway, Haskell's lawyers offered me a settlement and my lawyer told me to take it; after all, the guy didn't actually succeed in raping me, so how tough would the courts get on him? I got the picture. He was somebody. I wasn't.''

Determined to get the whole story, he urged, ''And...?''

''And I took the damned money! Okay? I needed to pay medical bills and rent and stuff until I could work again. And my parents weren't doing so great, not that they would ever say so. Both of my sisters have other responsibilities—kids to support. So I put most of the money in an account for my parent's retirement.''

But he could tell she wasn't okay with the fact that she'd backed down and had traded a possible conviction for money. ''Hey, sometimes you do what you have to, even if it's not your first choice.'' Just as he himself had learned.

"And then I didn't start working like I thought I would. I couldn't look at a Broadway theater marquee without thinking about what happened."

"So you came to Las Vegas, thinking you could make a fresh start."

She nodded. "JoJo's wedding was the excuse I needed." She laughed weakly. "So my first week here, my best friend disappears, someone follows me home . . . and now this."

Thinking he would have to stop his interrogation there, he asked, "You want to quit?"

"Not on your life. I have to find JoJo."

She'd finally involved the police, Nick knew. A detective had been questioning employees about JoJo that morning.

"JoJo'll probably be back from her honeymoon any day," Nick said dryly. Then would the blackmail begin?

"I don't think so. She called me last night."

His turn to tense. "From where?"

"I don't know. She was whispering like she didn't want someone to overhear. She pleaded for help, indicated she was being held against her will. Then nothing."

JoJo being held against her will? Maybe things weren't exactly as they'd seemed, Nick thought. Could he have been wrong?

"You have no idea where she was?"

"None. If only I had a way to get at the telephone company's records. . . . There'd be a record of the call and the number it came from."

"I might be able to arrange that."

"Don't you have to have a subpoena or something to get that kind of information?"

"If you don't have connections." Which he had via his father.

While Sasha sounded sleepy, she also sounded hopeful. "Nicky, are you saying you're going to help me find JoJo?"

He pulled her closer and stroked her hair, his arms banded tightly around her.

"That's what I'm saying."

His heart lurched as Sasha truly relaxed for the first time and snuggled against him as if she trusted him completely. She shouldn't, though.

What he wasn't saying was that he wanted to find JoJo Weston as much as Sasha did...to get back what she'd stolen from him.

SASHA WOKE through a haze, gray light spilling into the room. Her eyes flashed open. This wasn't her bedroom... rather, it wasn't JoJo's. It was Nick's.

And unless she was mistaken, Nick was curled around her spoon-fashion, and his hand was curled around her robe-covered breast.

The heavy weight on her sensitive flesh quickened her pulse. She lay still, her mind wakening fully, going over their conversation of the night before. Sometime after Nick had assured her he'd help her find JoJo, she must have fallen asleep.

And he'd had the nerve not only to put her in his bed, but to join her.

Unsure of exactly how she felt about the fact, she knew one thing for certain. She had every reason to be afraid. She hadn't gotten close to a man since the attack. And Nick might be even more dangerous than Dave Haskell.

Behind her, Nick stirred, groaning. His hand flexed around her breast, the terry scraping against her nipple and arousing Sasha instantly. Heat curled through her middle, and instinctively, she adjusted her hips. Nick was pressed tight against her bottom, and she was certain from the shape of things that he wasn't wearing any underwear.

Tentatively, so as not to wake him, she moved her hand back to check. Flesh stirred and she couldn't resist exploring more fully. The next thing she felt was an insistent nuzzling at her neck.

Nick was definitely awake.

"I should be going," she whispered lamely, snapping her hand back where it belonged.

"Mmm."

Her heart was hammering. How had she gotten herself into this situation?

"We both have things to do."

Though at the moment, with Nick's hand sliding across her chest to find its way inside the terry robe, she couldn't quite remember exactly what she had to do. He honed in on her breast, already tightened with excitement. His thumb stroked the nipple as he shifted so that he was half over her.

"If you're sure you want to leave...." he murmured.

Not knowing if she wanted this despite the heat inside her, not knowing if she should do this considering Nick's involvement with the murdered women—not to mention her best friend—Sasha hesitated. Lump in her throat, she stared up at the drop-dead gorgeous man who'd awakened her inner woman the first time she saw him.

Could she trust him?

Should she trust him?

He had possibly saved her life....

Still, a frisson of fear climbing up her spine, she truthfully said, "I'm not sure what I want, Nicky."

"Then try relaxing and see where this takes us."

His lips came down to feather her jaw. For a moment, she lost herself in the tingly sensation. Her entire body was alive and vibrant. Surely she wouldn't be feeling this way if she had any doubts about Nick. Still...

"We hardly know each other."

Working on her ear now, Nick said, "We know each other better than a lot of people know anyone."

Her eyes fluttered at the sensation and she had to choke out her words. "But I don't necessarily like everything I know about you."

That stopped him. He pulled back to face her, his hand leaving the folds of the robe. "What is it you think you know?"

She didn't like his tone or the way he was staring at her. His expression was a little scary. And the thought of admitting she knew about Mia and Glory made her mouth go dry and her stomach clench. If she brought up the murders, he would think she believed he was the guilty one. Not that she had any reason to believe he wasn't....

When she didn't answer, Nick asked, "Do you trust me?"

"I was just asking myself the same question."

"What kind of answer did you get?"

She stared into his face, searching for the truth. Something there scared her. A deep-seated anger. And yet...

"I *want* to trust you."

That was the heart of the truth, despite the fact that he made her afraid at times.

"Good. A good start."

Nick kissed her then, and Sasha didn't argue. Turning, she managed to slide under him more fully. She ran her hands over his shoulders and down his back, his musculature taut beneath his smooth skin. His tongue slipping against hers reminded her of a more intimate joining. Her belly tightened and her hips arched in response.

With a sexy groan, Nick broke the kiss. "If you're going to leave, now would be a good time."

His features were taut with desire and his eyes fathomless with passion. He could have just seduced her into staying, but he was giving her the choice. Part of her wished he hadn't left it up to her, but had continued on until she had no will. Now she had to make a rational decision, but how could she?

Did she trust him? She didn't know. Did she fear him? At times, definitely. Did she want him? Always.

And maybe that was the most important truth.

Instinct, rather than rationale, made her say, "I want to stay here with you."

He kissed her again, his hand delving back into the robe, this time opening it. He explored her fully, making her head spin, similar to the way it had the night before. Only this time, she was getting drunk on him. When he broke the kiss again, a sound of frustration escaped her.

Nick laughed and, rolling, pulled her up over him. Drugged with building desire, Sasha willingly straddled his hips. His hand flashed between her thighs. His fingers found her and within seconds she was wet and ready for whatever he had to offer.

Mind spinning with erotic flashes, she lost herself in a way she never had before. She'd always believed in knowing a man inside and out before getting close. She feared she didn't know the real Nick Donatelli at all. And yet, her instincts made her hope that, whatever else he might be, he wasn't a murderer. Throwing her head back, she moved against his hand, realizing that, ever so slowly, he was slipping a finger deep inside her.

A moment of pleasure and she was so close to the edge that she had to bite back a cry.

Removing his hand, Nick joined them fully. Sasha fell forward, her hands clutching the pillow on either side of his head. He took the tip of one breast into his mouth and suckled her until her hips rocked by instinct. His mouth urging her into a frenzy, she rode him hard. Her senses on overload, Sasha plunged over the edge, her cry echoed by his.

Only in the midst of free-fall did she wonder if she would live long enough to make love with Nick again.

Chapter Ten

Having made love twice more, once while showering, Sasha insisted, "I have to go."

Nick tried to detain her, yet again, but she slipped out of his soapy grasp. "To do what?" he asked.

"Get some rest, for one."

He raised a dark eyebrow. "You can do that here."

"Hah! With you around, I think not." She grabbed a towel and started drying off. "Besides, I figured I'd look through JoJo's things again, see if I can't get a clue as to her mystery groom's identity." Though she wasn't too hopeful about finding anything new, she had to do *something*. "And you have the phone call to follow up on, right?"

"Right."

"Promise?"

"Promise." He stuck his head out of the shower. "And Sasha, be careful. Someone tried to hurt you last night."

Someone other than Nick, she reassured herself. "Maybe it was nothing more than a prank."

"And maybe someone wanted your nose out of the way permanently."

Not that Nick had at any time suggested involving the authorities, she thought uneasily.

She gave him a last quick kiss and went in search of the clothes she'd retrieved from the dryer earlier. After slipping into them, she ran a wide-tooth comb through her damp hair, declining to worry about makeup for once.

As she headed for the front door, Nick's muffled off-key singing made her smile.

Halfway out the door, she screeched to a dead stop when she spotted Gaines VanDerZanden at the other end of the corridor. The high roller was leaving a suite across from the one where the big game had been held. He was using a key to lock the door behind him.

No doubt a dead-bolt key.

Sasha backed into Nick's apartment, his faint baritone telling her he was still preoccupied in the bath. Ear to the door that she'd left cracked open, she listened to the elevator arriving. At the same time, she dug for the rhinestone-studded key ring in her bag. The damn thing had to fit some lock in the hotel. Maybe it was his. When she was certain Gaines was gone, she cautiously opened the door. All clear. She sneaked down the hall, hoping that no one would come out of another suite.

Only when she held the key to the lock did it occur to her that Gaines might not have been alone, that he, too, might have left someone behind. Her pulse raced at the thought of being discovered. She palmed the key and knocked lightly, praying that no one would answer, thinking that if someone did, she could always say she was looking for Gaines.

But no one seemed to be about, thank heavens.

Sasha sighed with relief and resumed her activity. When the key slid into the lock's opening easily, she was elated...for a moment. And then she was disappointed when the thing wouldn't turn. Wondering if the cut could be rough, she adjusted accordingly, moving it this way and that. But no matter how she tried, the key wouldn't budge.

She stared at the door for another moment, willing it to open, but no such luck. The key went back into her bag to await another try. So what did this mean? That Gaines was off the hook?

Thoughtful, she turned from the door only to come face-to-face with Vito Tolentino. That gave her a good jolt. She hadn't heard the elevator deliver him, but he was standing between it and Nick's apartment. His expression was not reassuring. Had he seen what she'd been doing?

Hoping not, she bluffed, heading for the elevator as though he weren't scowling at her. She even managed a polite smile as she started to pass him.

"Not so fast."

His gravelly voice stopped Sasha in her tracks. She thought quickly. Desperately.

"What is it?"

"What were you doing there?" His voice was soft and filled with suspicion.

"That's Gaines VanDerZanden's suite, isn't it?"

"What if it is?"

"He sent me some flowers after the show last night." She figured the truth was her best alibi. "I wanted to thank him in person."

"You came all the way up for that?"

She arched her eyebrows at him meaningfully. "If you want to know why I'm here, ask Nicky...Mr. D."

His stare was measuring. Then he nodded. "I heard about your *accident*."

"You wouldn't happen to know who was responsible, would you?"

Vito's expression darkened. "What makes you think such a thing?"

"You're always around."

"I work for Mr. D."

"And his father before him," she said, reaching out to press the elevator button. "Nicky told me you kept an eye on things when Sally was . . . away."

"If I hadn't, Carmine Scudella woulda sucked him dry."

Scudella. There was that name again. Sasha was surprised she hadn't made the connection between Mia and Carmine, whom she'd read about in JoJo's newspaper clippings.

"It's good to know you were around, then."

"I'd do anything for the Donatellis."

Anything? Including murdering women who rejected Nick?

While Sasha could hardly believe anyone was that devoted an employee, the idea was planted. She determined to find out all she could about Vito Tolentino . . . but from whom?

A *ding* was followed by the elevator doors opening. "Ah, my chariot awaits," she joked, stepping into the car.

Vito was still staring as the elevator doors closed between them.

And Sasha was still thinking.

Maybe she should find out more, not only about Vito, but about the Scudella family, as well. And who better to tell her than Sally Donatelli himself? Foolish as the action might be, she decided to pay Nick's father a visit. Nick admitted he hadn't been frequenting *Don-*

atelli's, so she shouldn't fear running into him. The only concern she had was whether or not the owner would be there so early, before she had to report for the first show.

And whether or not Sally would be glad enough to see her to keep her visit to himself.

"To what do I owe this pleasure?" Sally asked when the maître d' brought Sasha to his table.

"My pleasure. The food's wonderful and a girl's got to eat, right?"

A speculative gleam in the green eyes so like his son's, he said, "So sit."

"I don't want to bother you," she fudged, relieved that neither Caroline nor Vito was anywhere in sight. The fact that either of them might have been there came as an afterthought, too late to stop her. "I just wanted to say hello."

"No bother. A man would be a fool to dine alone when he could break bread with a lovely woman."

Sasha didn't fight it. She had what she wanted. She slid into the curved booth, keeping a comfortable distance from the owner. She planned to hype her personal interest in Nick to his father. See where that would get her.

As he had the other night, Sally ordered for both of them. Even though she had less than two hours before the first show, Sasha ate a goodly portion of squid in a butter-and-garlic sauce, followed by ravioli stuffed with polenta and topped with pesto. And throughout the meal, Sally kept her so busy talking about her career that Sasha never got a chance to pump him.

After dinner, while they sipped at cappuccinos, Sally asked, "So why are you really here?"

"I told you—"

"A fairy tale. That's okay. You wanted to see me. Why?"

Prepared for his suspicion, she said, "All right, you got me. I guess I wanted to know more about Nicky."

His gaze was penetrating. "You're serious about Nick. You want to know if he's like his old man?"

The truth too close for comfort, she lightly said, "He's definitely got his father's looks."

"But you're interested in whether or not he's got his father's...business acumen?"

A careful way of putting things.

"Nicky told me he took over for you until you, uh, were able to get back to business," she said just as carefully.

"I was incarcerated for eighteen years. I did my time. My business is mostly legal now."

She didn't miss the *mostly*. "I wasn't wondering about you."

"You want to know if Nick is on the up-and-up."

Sasha did want to know and figured Sally probably really did think she wanted the information for personal purposes. "Is he?"

"Something you should ask him."

"Will he tell me the truth?"

"He won't lie to a woman he cares about."

But how would she know if he was truthful because he cared, or lying because he didn't? Sally's statement gave her the opening she needed.

"Did Nicky really love Mia...or did he get involved with her because Carmine was seeing to your interests?"

"He cared. And he got involved *despite* her father."

So Carmine was Mia's father, she thought, storing away that nugget of information. "I heard she had a brother. Did he object, too?"

"Hard to say. He was a guest of the government for quite a while before Mia and Nick got involved. I doubt he had much to say about the relationship."

Sasha was trying to figure out what part, if any, of this information would be useful. She was just about to work Vito into the conversation, when a beaded purse slammed onto the table before her. Startled, she stared into Caroline Donatelli's furious expression.

"You're telling this stranger about Nick and Mia? Papa, what's wrong with you?"

Sally's mild manner disappeared. "You're telling me I gotta answer to my daughter about who I can talk to... and about what?"

Caroline swallowed hard and regrouped. "No, Papa, of course not. I was startled, that's all."

"You're late."

"I'm sorry. I had something to take care of. But I see you haven't been lonely."

Sasha's cue to leave. She rose and smiled at Sally. "I loved the meal. Thank you. I need to get to the showroom."

"Give Nick our love," Caroline said sweetly.

Having no intention of telling Nick any such thing—hoping his sister would keep her mouth shut—Sasha merely smiled agreeably as she left.

Had the intrusion on Nick's father been worth the effort? Hard to say. She felt as if there must be a piece of the puzzle in all that information, but she didn't know the important stuff from the filler. And what did Nick's family background have to do with JoJo?

The conversation was replaying through her head as she swept through the casino. Across the room she spotted Mac, who signaled for her to wait, and gave over his blackjack table to another dealer. Then he rushed to join her.

"I'm on break and I need to talk to you. Can you spare a few minutes?"

From Mac's grim expression, she didn't think this was merely another attempt to get her to see him, so Sasha said, "Sure."

A few minutes later, they were settled in a booth of the Coral Reef Bar, colas before them. Mac wasted no time in getting to the point.

"I hear you had some trouble last night. That you went for a dip in the showroom tank."

Sasha gulped down a mouthful of her soda. "Good grief, is it all over the casino?"

"This is a small community. Any kind of unusual news spreads fast. So, what happened?"

Chances were he already knew, so Sasha saw no point in hedging. "I went for an involuntary swim—someone pushed me in."

Mac slammed his fist on the booth's table. "Donatelli is dangerous!"

Flabbergasted by what was close to a direct accusation, Sasha asked, "You think he pushed me in, then rescued me?"

"He's done a hell of a lot worse."

"You know him that well?" she asked, remembering he'd warned her off Nick before.

"I know *of* him. I know what happened to Mia Scudella and Glory Hale. I warned JoJo, too, but she wouldn't listen. Now, who knows what happened to her."

He sounded as if he actually cared. A shiver shot through Sasha and she stared down into her soda, suddenly unsure of her actions with Nick. She'd made love to him. Dear Lord, she hoped she hadn't fooled herself.

"JoJo's all right." When he gave her a peculiar look, she added, "At least I hope so." Noting how his expression changed subtly. "At any rate, I intend to continue looking for her."

"You're putting yourself in danger."

"I don't care," she said heatedly. "JoJo has been my best friend for a lot of years. She was there for me when I needed her. I'll find her if it's the last thing I ever do."

Mac sat back and studied her for a minute. "I guess you have to do what you have to do. Listen, if you ever need help, you find me."

"I know where the blackjack tables are," she said more brightly than she was feeling.

"I'm not kidding. And if I'm not here, you can find me in the Groves," he said, naming an apartment complex that was a bit fancier than JoJo's and a few blocks closer to the Caribbean. "I'm in the building directly to the left of the entrance. Apartment 4."

Spooked by his seriousness, she said, "I appreciate the offer. Hopefully, I'll never have to use it." She stood. "I need to get going." She intended to use this time to figure out which was JoJo's locker, get into it any way she could, and search it before anyone else showed.

"Break a leg."

Sasha said, "Thanks," and moved off. She felt Mac's gaze follow her all the way to the showroom.

Inside, the house, as well as the stage, was dimly lit and empty as she had expected. The tank stood there, recessed, mocking her. She faltered at the top of the stairs, the memory of being pushed into the tank vivid after the discussion she'd just had.

But Nick couldn't have done it, she told herself. Not any more than he'd murdered those women, or was responsible for JoJo's disappearance.

And yet . . . Mac seemed awfully sure of himself.

A creak behind her sent Sasha spinning around, heart thundering, to search the area. A movement alerted her. Then Lester Perkins separated from the shadows. She eyed the maintenance man warily and wondered if he'd been there all along. If so, why hadn't he said something immediately?

He shoved at his glasses, but they still rested crooked on his nose. "You're all right."

Pulse slowing, she said, "Why wouldn't I be?"

"After taking a dive into that tank . . . uh, Mr. D told me to fish your earring outta the water."

He patted the pockets of his uniform, then, finding the right one, pulled out the crystal shoulder duster. She took it from him and gave it a once-over.

"Thanks. It doesn't look any worse for the wear," she said, slipping it into her shoulder bag. "I guess the water didn't hurt it."

"That's 'cause it wasn't in the water."

"Where then?"

"One level down."

"In the props area?" Wondering what Lester had been doing on the lower levels, Sasha asked, "How?"

"The elevator wasn't settled all the way in place and the earring got through the crack."

The old showroom had two such stage elevators and a turntable—whole sections of floor that could rise or descend to the lower basement levels—and a *band-*

wagon that not only lowered and lifted, but could even move horizontally. The steel tracks with their subtly raised metal edges on the stage, including the moving platforms, could be hazardous to an unwary performer. And could be the reason the elevator holding the swimmer's tank hadn't closed properly—perhaps some metal part had come free and was interfering.

Considering Lester wore such thick glasses, Sasha was amazed that small details like a crack between elevator and stage didn't get by him. "You must be pretty observant."

"I do my best."

She wondered if the maintenance man was observant in other areas, as well. "Lester, you said you worked for the Donatellis for years, right?" Somehow, she knew the key to everything was buried in the past.

"Just about forever."

"Maybe you'll remember when Nicky got engaged to Mia Scudella, then. Was it before or after he took over Sally's business interests from her father?"

Lester took a step back. "What are you asking me about Mia for?"

Why was he so put out? "It's a simple question."

"Well I don't know nothing."

Thinking that he did know, and wondering what he was trying to avoid telling her, she insisted, "But you were working for the family at the time."

To no avail. Lester turned his back on her and stalked off, muttering to himself about people sticking their noses where they didn't belong. Taken aback by his rudeness, Sasha clenched her jaw so she wouldn't say something equally unkind about his behavior. Just as he had appeared from the shadows, he slipped back into them and vanished, probably into a maintenance closet,

Sasha guessed . . . though she swore she could still feel his gaze on her.

Remembering his penchant for show girls, Sasha shook off the uncomfortable sensation that it gave her.

Lester Perkins certainly was an odd one, if loyal to the family he'd worked for all his life, which was undoubtedly the reason he didn't want to talk about the past.

She checked her watch. Still early. No one around. Not even the technicians or stagehands. It would be a while, at least a quarter of an hour, before people began filtering in. From experience, she knew that once a show was set, the cast and crew pretty much arrived at the last minute unless otherwise ordered by the producer. She figured she had just enough time to get at that locker.

She descended into the showroom, her attention once more drawn to the water tank.

For the first time, Sasha really allowed herself to think about what had happened the night before, to speculate more fully about who could have been responsible for her accident. And why. Maybe the incident had been no more than a prank, as she'd suggested to Nick. The motive could be as simple as retribution for a little jealousy—something of which Barbie Doll was fully capable. Or rejection—she had several candidates there, including Mac Schneider. But the blackjack dealer had seemed genuinely concerned about her welfare.

She found herself ascending the steps to the stage apron, staring at the tank as if it held the answers.

What if, as Nick had indicated, someone wanted to get rid of her permanently, before she delved too deeply into JoJo's disappearance?

Had Nick been talking about himself?

Soft sounds interrupted her thoughts. Sasha whipped around, but despite her suspicion that she was not alone, she couldn't spot anyone. Lester, again?

The sounds continued, snagging her attention. Sasha frowned at the muffled tapping. Where in the world could that be coming from? She listened more closely, as she neared the bandwagon that had been lowered to the first basement level, about thirteen feet below.

Who'd been fooling with the mechanical device? she wondered. All had been level with the stage the night before when she'd searched for her earring.

Some crew member had to be in one of the sets and props storage areas preparing something for the show. Lights were on—the lower floor glowed dimly.

About to go on to the dressing room, she realized the tapping sounds were not random. She focused her attention on them and picked up a distinctive pattern. Five taps, a long pause, then two more taps.

Tap-tap-tap-tap-tap . . . tap-tap.

Realizing the significance, Sasha froze to the spot and listened harder, wanting to be certain.

Tap-tap-tap-tap-tap . . . tap-tap.

Her pulse rushed through her veins. That was it, all right. *JoJo's signal.* JoJo always knocked or rang the doorbell in that cadence ever since Sasha had to avoid a pesty neighbor who'd had a thing for her and would just show up. If she forgot her keys or had her hands full, JoJo had used the signal to let Sasha know it was only her.

Tap-tap-tap-tap-tap . . . tap-tap.

Dear Lord, JoJo was down there somewhere!

Sasha looked around frantically. Spotting the nearest trapdoor that led below, she wasted no time in taking up the chase. She left the stage and descended a narrow ladder-like set of steps to the first basement.

The shadowy expanse held a maze of sets and props in place for the current show. And behind them were myriad storage areas that she knew nothing about. While she'd been down here for rehearsals and the shows the evening before, she'd only gone from the backstage stairs to one of the stage elevators and vice versa.

"JoJo?" she called softly, her skin pebbling with the creepiness of the situation. She didn't like being down here alone...if she was alone. She rubbed her bare arms and called again. "JoJo?"

No one answered. The muffled tapping sounds had stopped for the moment, leaving Sasha at a loss as to where to begin her search.

Swallowing hard, she moved forward, trying to look in every direction at once. She wasn't going to be caught unaware again. Above, its red "on" button glowing, a camera watched her silently. She knew the various cameras dotting the basement were meant to prevent accidents—giving crew members in the technical booth a view of the two basement levels when using the mechanical devices.

Suddenly, a whirring and a jerk told her the platform she was standing on was being put into use now, probably being brought back up into position where it belonged at the beginning of the show. Caught in the middle of the ascending bandwagon, she raced to the edge, thinking to jump off.

But the platform had gone too far, was already several feet in the air, so she backed off.

"Damn!"

She'd wait until it rose to stage level, then use the trapdoor steps to get back down to resume her search.

Halfway there, the bandwagon jerked to a stop. Sasha teetered on her high heels and swore softly. Had the technician seen her on camera? Though that would be no reason to stop the platform halfway to its destination.

Her head came nearly to the opening, and she could see all around the stage. Empty.

"Hey!" she yelled. "Anyone around?"

Her only answer was a grinding of gears, alerting her to possible danger. The bandwagon was shifting horizontally now, moving toward the rear end of the stage. Her stomach clenched and a slight sweat broke out over her skin. Normally, anyone transported this way would be sitting so as not to be anywhere near the beams and steel rails overhead.

So Sasha sat.

And a moment later, the bandwagon stopped dead.

"What now?"

With the platform fully tucked under the stage, she felt entombed, cut off from all but a faint light. A thrill of warning shot through her, but she tried to ignore the fear, tried to keep her focus on finding JoJo. How long before she could resume her search?

Suddenly realizing she hadn't heard the tapping in quite a while, Sasha wondered how she would even find her friend.

"Double damn!"

Frustrated, she thought to jump from the platform. Maybe she could remain sitting and swing herself off or something. But when she tried to move, she couldn't. Not in the mood for another delay, she groaned.

"Now what?"

Upon inspection, she found that a piece of metal held her knit dress to the platform. Part of the track system for the elevators had come loose and attached itself to her solidly. She was wearing a new dress and didn't want to ruin it, so she carefully began working it free, even as another sound of gears shifting alerted her to a new threat.

She glanced behind her. The turntable descended several feet and stopped, though it continued to rotate, reminding her of a giant saw. And the bandwagon started up again, moving directly toward it. What was going on? Someone who didn't know what he was doing was messing around with potentially dangerous equipment.

"Hey!" she yelled, waving her arms at the nearest camera. "Someone stop this thing!"

But neither the bandwagon nor the rotating disk stopped. And something told Sasha that this was no accident. That someone meant her to be trapped.

Hurt.

Perhaps killed.

It came to her then that that same someone had wanted her to think JoJo was around, when really she wasn't. Someone who knew about the tapping had used it to lure her into the basement. Someone who had reason to want her out of the way, Sasha realized grimly. Fighting disappointment that her friend wasn't around to be rescued, after all, she ripped her dress free and, on hands and knees, scrambled to the edge of the platform, yelling toward the opening in the stage.

"Hey! If anyone's up there, stop the damn elevators! Is anyone there?"

A glance over her shoulder told her the edge of the bandwagon was now sliding under the turntable. Her head grew light and she fought dizziness. Fought panic. *Stay calm,* she ordered herself. *Don't lose your head— think!*

She had two choices. Either she would have to lie flat so there would be enough room for her between the two platforms, or she would have to get off. Once she was sandwiched under the rotating turntable, she realized she would be a sitting duck—that she could be crushed to death as easily as a pesty fly. Sasha knew she really had no choice, after all.

She looked down. Swallowed hard. She faced a good six-foot jump from a moving platform to a cement floor. She was shaking, having a difficult time controlling her limbs, but she managed to dangle her legs over the edge and remove her shoes. Then she turned over and slid onto her stomach, backing off the device until the tops of her thighs were free of the surface. Praying she wouldn't break a leg—the ground was now a mere three or four feet from her toes—she was about to slip off carefully, when the platform came to another jerking stop.

And, out of control, Sasha went flying off backward.

Chapter Eleven

The breath knocked right out of her, Sasha sprawled across the cement floor for a moment, so stunned she couldn't move. Then, realizing she was in mortal danger, she ignored her protesting limbs, scrambled to her feet and made for the mouth of the trapdoor.

"Sasha!"

Nick's voice, coming from that very opening, froze her to the spot. Her mind raced . . . directly to the worst assumptions. Of course, Nick would know all of Jo-Jo's habits, including her signal, she thought, watching him descend the stairs fast. Sasha knew she had to find another way out if she wanted to escape, yet she was unable to force herself to move.

"Hey, are you all right?" he demanded.

Nick Donatelli was face-to-face with her now, coming for her. Trembling, Sasha shook her head.

"No!" she protested weakly, the stuffing knocked out of her more from the realization that the man she'd made love with might have done this to her, rather than from the brutal fall itself. "Stay away from me."

But the protest was muffled against his shoulder as Nick gathered her in his arms. Without a clue as to what she was supposed to think now, she held herself stiff.

Two days in a row she'd had potentially deadly accidents. Two days in a row, Nick had made a timely appearance. Coincidence? Or a cleverly thought-out plan?

"My God," Nick murmured into her hair, "when I heard your voice and realized you were in trouble..."

He didn't finish. And she didn't know whether or not to believe him. He was stroking her head with one hand, her spine with the other. Trying to soothe away her suspicions? Her deepest emotions responded to him, but she concentrated on getting to the truth.

"You stopped the bandwagon?" she asked.

"As soon as I could. When I heard you yell, I rushed up to the technical booth. The door was wide open and the booth was empty, but all the equipment was on. I saw you on one of the monitors." He moved her away from him but didn't let go of her arms. "What the hell are you doing down here, anyway?"

"Looking for JoJo."

"What?"

"I heard tapping," she said, studying him carefully as she vocalized. "Da-da-da-da-da...da-da."

He swore and muttered, "No wonder...who could have known about that silly knock of hers?"

"You did."

As if finally realizing why she hadn't loosened up under his ministrations, why she hadn't thrown herself into his arms and thanked him for coming to her rescue once more, he said, "I'm not even going to respond to that." Though his grim visage was reaction enough. "You're in shock. C'mon, let's get you some air."

Nick pushed her toward the narrow steps. Sasha stumbled up, aware that he was barely a breath behind her. She sensed his searing anger. Would he really be angry if he were the one? And if he had tried to kill her, why hadn't he finished the job?

Once onto the stage, she found a possible answer to the second question. Witnesses. Several people stood around as if waiting to see what was going on. Yale Riker. Crew members she didn't know, yet. Barbie Doll. While a concerned-looking Yale approached, the other dancer remained in the background, her features passive.

"Darling, whatever happened to you?" Yale demanded, wide-eyed as he took in her disheveled appearance. "What were you doing in the basement?"

Before she could answer, Nick did so for her. "She was exploring and got into some hot water. But everything is fine now."

"Thank God! I don't know what I would do if anything happened to my new star!"

"I'm all right," Sasha told him, although the hip she'd landed on already nagged at her when she walked. Since she didn't carry painkillers of any kind herself, she hoped someone did. She'd be visibly bruised, too, and by the next day would probably need a liberal amount of body makeup to disguise the fact.

Arm around her shoulders, Nick led her toward the dressing rooms, past Barbie, who for once couldn't conceal her true feelings. As she looked into gray eyes filled with hatred, Sasha shuddered...and wondered if Barbie had known about JoJo's signal.

Convenient that the other dancer was present...as she had been minutes before Sasha had taken that unexpected dive into the tank. Could Barbie be jealous enough to kill? Then why was JoJo still alive?

At least she prayed nothing more *permanent* had happened to her friend.

By the time Nick got her away from prying eyes and ears, Sasha was beginning to feel guilty for suspecting him. She should be grateful he'd been around to respond to her cry for help. He pulled her into in a private corner of the backstage area opposite the hall leading to the dressing rooms. His hand on her arm scorched her.

Even now, with all her emotions in turmoil, he had the power to make her want him.

"I think I should keep you some place safe," he said, seeming to have forgotten about her earlier insinuation.

She met his gaze steadily and, with more bravery than she was feeling, she told him, "I'm not going into hiding."

His visage darkened again. "Not even when someone's trying to hurt you?"

"Not even then." She felt like telling him she could take care of herself, but all he had to do was look at her to put a lie to her words. "I must be getting close, Nicky, or this wouldn't have happened. Whoever has JoJo has a bad case of nerves."

And she realized that discussing this with him meant she didn't really believe he was guilty. Or didn't want to. Certainly that. For Sasha was coming to terms with a disturbing fact. She had some heavy duty feelings for Nick Donatelli—feelings she didn't want to put a name to—and after suspecting she would never be able to care for a man again. What a rotten trick life had played on her. Why Nick? He wasn't the kind of guy who was looking for commitment, and she wasn't the type of woman who would stay in a relationship where commitment wasn't at least a possibility.

"I hope to have an answer soon," he said.

She blinked. "Answer?"

"JoJo's call."

Sasha took a big breath. In all the tumult, she'd forgotten about his promise to have someone track down those records. Now it became the one bright spot in her present. She couldn't help feeling like something of a failure after five days of spinning her wheels. If she found JoJo because of the phone call, she would owe this, too, to Nick.

"I only hope we're in time," she murmured.

"All we can do is hope."

She looked up into his intense green gaze and nodded. "Yes, hope."

Hope that JoJo was still alive. Hope that Nick had nothing to do with her friend's disappearance. Hope that he hadn't killed Mia Scudella or Glory Hale. Hope that he hadn't been the one terrorizing her.

Indeed, she did have a lot to hope for.

He stroked his knuckles against her cheek and, for a moment, revealed a side of himself that she had never seen before. For a moment, the fierce, mocking Nick Donatelli appeared open and vulnerable. Why? Because of her? Or because he feared what she might learn?

"Oh, Nicky." Wishing she knew the truth about him, she allowed his name to escape her like a sigh.

"Sasha."

Fingers threading through her hair, Nick anchored her and pulled her closer. His kiss was deep and demanding, as if he were trying to impress her with that which she could not readily believe. As if he were trying to obliterate all the rumor and speculation and give to her the truth she needed.

Overwhelmed, Sasha sank against him, clenching the lapels of his white suit as if grabbing a fleeting opportunity with both hands. She poured all her crazy, mixed-up emotions into that single kiss because she feared she might not have the chance otherwise.

The slight contact of her body against his provoked the memories of their night together. Flashes of him below her, above her, behind her played across her mind. Her breasts tightened...a knot ripened low in her belly...a wet warmth gathered between her thighs.

She wanted him...needed him...ached for him...

But who knew if they would ever be together again?

Floating, lost in the moment, Sasha was startled when Nick broke the kiss and sat her away from him.

"Time for you to get ready, if that's really what you want."

Gathering her control, ignoring the pulsing in her woman's center, she looked beyond his shoulder. Stagehands and technicians swirled all along the backstage area, preparing for the night's first performance.

"That's what I have to do," she said.

Nick let her go. "I'll be around," he promised.

Making her way through the hallway, she tried not to limp. But the first thing she did upon entering the dressing room was to find a couple extra-strength aspirins. Then, realizing that most of the dancers were already in costume, she went to fetch hers from the rack. And couldn't find it.

"Did someone grab the wrong costume?" she yelled, hoping the person had merely neglected to return it.

A chorus of "no"s set her to searching all the racks in the room in case she'd misplaced it. But no, hers was gone all right. How could a costume have just disappeared? Instinct whipped her around, made her search the room for Barbie, but the blonde was nowhere to be seen.

Furious, thinking the jealous dancer might have sabotaged her, she asked the dresser, "Do you have another costume somewhere around here that might fit me?"

"Afraid not," the efficient woman said. "If you could get your hands on JoJo Weston's costume, you might be able to squeeze into it."

The name hit her like a jolt. "What do you mean? Someone took JoJo's costume, too?"

"Don't think so. She was always sticking things in her locker, forgetting to hang them up again."

"Her locker." Every time Sasha had started out to find it, something had interrupted. "Which one?"

Leading Sasha back to the locker area, the dresser pointed out JoJo's. "Good luck getting it open."

Sasha grinned. She didn't need luck. The lock was the four-digit, self-programmable kind. And since JoJo always said she was lucky that she remembered her own birthday, Sasha was certain that the combination she'd used forever hadn't changed.

She tried two-eight-six-four. The lock popped like a charm. She opened the door. Inside, JoJo's costume hung from a hook.

"Mess with me, will you?" she muttered, thinking of the look Barbie had given her.

Sasha grabbed the showroom version of a skimpy latex swimming costume, including a spangly, see-through cover-up, which was caught on whatever was stuffed in the bottom of the locker. Sasha set to righting the situation, freeing the material from a makeup bag JoJo had left there. Then, thinking she should look through JoJo's things now, before she lost the opportunity again, she set the costume down.

She flipped open the bag and removed a wig and several hairpieces. Makeup was jumbled across the bottom. Pancake. Eye shadows. Blushers. Lipsticks. She checked one of the side pockets filled with hair clips and combs. Opening the other, about to give up, her eyes caught a sudden gleam as light shot into the pocket.

She dug around and brought up yet another hair accessory...but one that didn't belong to JoJo.

Sasha recognized the distinctive design...the real diamonds and emeralds, one of which was missing from its setting.

No wonder Caroline Donatelli had taken to the "Veronica Lake look," as Sally had called it.

So what had JoJo been doing with her property?

Closing her friend's locker, a sick feeling inside, she slipped the comb into her own bag. Nick had accused JoJo of stealing something other than money. Had this been it? What was the significance?

The question ate at her as she made a quick change. The lights blinked, signaling five minutes until show time.

A fast makeup job and Sasha was backstage with the other performers. She immediately spied Barbie, waiting to go on with several other dancers. Fury guiding her, Sasha approached the blonde and whipped her around.

The gray eyes widened guiltily.

"That's what I thought." Sasha pulled Barbie off to the side, muttering, "So you thought you could get away with this."

"It was a joke, for Pete's sake." But the blonde was appropriately nervous at being caught. "Haven't you ever played practical jokes on the new kid?"

"I'm not a kid and neither are you," Sasha told her as the show's intro music began to play. Testing to see what reaction it would bring, she added, "And that stunt you pulled with the bandwagon and turntable really wasn't funny."

"What stunt?" Then, as Sasha's meaning dawned on her, Barbie's expression changed to one of horror. "I had nothing to do with that. Honest."

And Sasha thought she might be crazy, but she believed the other woman. Barbie was mean-spirited, capable of pranks, but Sasha doubted she was capable of murder. Sasha had no more time to question her, for half the show girls were already on stage. Barbie stumbled by her and shoved into place just in time to make her entrance. Following up the rear, Sasha was able to take her time and gather her wits before going on.

She gave a terrific performance, not missing a beat, even though only one thing preyed on her mind.

What in the world was the significance of JoJo having Caroline's comb?

HAVING LEARNED MUCH MORE than he'd set out to discover that night, Nick waited for Sasha outside the dressing room. Other show girls drifted out two and three at a time. When Barbie passed him, she averted her face and hurried on her way. He hardly noticed. As usual, Sasha was taking her time. Nick was hard-pressed to keep a handle on his temper and not burst into the dressing room to demand an explanation.

Finally, the last few girls straggled out, Sasha among them. Spotting him immediately, she took her leave of the other dancers.

"Hi, have any news?" she asked a bit too brightly.

He had news, all right. News that made him want to throttle her. "Dressing room empty?" he asked tersely.

She gave him a weird look. "Yeah. I was among the last out, as usual."

He placed a hand on the small of her back and, ignoring the way she stiffened, steered her back inside.

"Hey, what's the big idea?" she demanded, seeming more nervous than indignant.

And no wonder. She had reason to eye him warily.

"You got a problem with me?" he asked.

She licked her lips and ignored the question. "So what did you find out? About the *phone call?*" she emphasized.

"The call was traced to a cellular phone."

She didn't try masking her disappointment. "Then it could have come from anywhere."

"Yale Riker's phone."

"Omigod!" She dropped her shoulder bag on a bench and recouped. "Yale's been going on about his phone being missing. But that happened after I started working here, so I doubt it went too far."

The producer and his phone receding in importance for the moment, Nick coldly said, "*You* went too far tonight, Sasha. What was the idea of going to see my father behind my back?"

She squirmed. "I needed to find out something."

"And did you?" He knew she'd been pumping his father about Mia, damn her.

"I'm not sure. So who squealed?"

"Caroline told me."

She didn't seem surprised. "Figures. Caroline—"

"Don't start on my sister!"

"Why not? She loves using *me* as a target."

"Let's drop Caroline."

"Let's not." Taking a big breath, Sasha reached into a zippered compartment of her shoulder bag. "Recognize this?" She pulled out the elusive comb with the missing emerald.

Nick went very still. He hadn't been prepared for this. Hadn't been prepared for Sasha being in cahoots with JoJo. Once again, a woman he cared for had betrayed him. Only this time, it hurt twice as bad.

"Is this where you present the blackmail message?" he asked wryly.

"What?"

"From JoJo. You're in on this with her, right?"

Her face pulled into a puzzled frown. She was good. He'd give her that.

"Nicky, I don't know what you're talking about."

"Don't *Nicky* me."

He advanced on her and, fear flashing across her features, she backed into the makeup counter. He kept going, until he was certain she could feel his breath on her face. She leaned away from him. Had the audacity to appear angry, when he was the one who'd been played for a fool. Again.

"You said JoJo stole from you." She held the comb practically in his face. "This was it, right?"

He grabbed it from her. "Not too bright, Sasha. Without this, your plan won't work, will it?"

"What plan?" she practically shouted.

He moved closer so that the length of his body was against hers. Even now, with this betrayal between them, she set him on fire. She leaned even farther back.

Fisted hands on the counter, the teeth of the comb pressing into his palm, he leaned over her so she couldn't miss his message.

"Don't mess with me, Sasha. That wouldn't be a good thing for you." He watched sudden fear cut through her, but he couldn't revel in the knowledge. "Tell me the truth. Were you in on this with JoJo all along?"

She frantically shoved at his chest, but he refused to budge.

"There was no plan, damn you!" she ground out. "When I went for my opening-number costume, it was gone. The dresser said I might be able to use JoJo's if I could figure out how to get into her locker. So I did. The comb was the bonus. I have no idea why JoJo had it."

Warily, he stared deep into her eyes, searching for the truth. All he could find there was righteous indignation. Thinking that maybe he'd jumped to the wrong conclusion, that maybe she really had found the comb just as she'd said, he backed off.

"All right." He pinned her with his gaze as she straightened. "If you swear this is the truth, I'll try to believe it."

"Don't do me any favors!"

Cursing his quick temper, Nick said, "Sasha—"

But she cut him off. "No. Don't *Sasha* me," she said, echoing him. "Take the damn comb and get out!"

He gave her a mocking smile. "This place is mine, remember?"

"Fine. *I'll* go!"

She grabbed her bag and Nick grabbed her. "You're not going anywhere until we get this settled."

"So help me, you'd better let go of me—"

"Or you'll what?"

"I'll make you. Or I'll die trying."

Knowing she meant it, her pulse visible in her slender throat, he let go. "Maybe we both need to cool down."

"I don't want to cool down. I just want to get away from you. For good," she added.

"You're angry. You don't mean that."

"Don't I?" Storming out of the locker room, she muttered, "How stupid could I be getting myself into a relationship with a man who might be a murderer!"

Nick clenched his jaw and threw a fist into the mirror. Thankfully it didn't break, not that his luck was anything to brag on. He opened his hand, stared down at the incriminating comb. He thumbed the empty setting where the missing emerald should be. *Damn Caroline!* Slipping the evidence into his pocket, he counted slowly to ten and went after Sasha. She was moving fast, out of the showroom before he could play catch-up. He took the steps two at a time. Threw open the door...and saw her talking with Gaines VanDer-Zanden a distance away.

Nick stopped short and stared.

He became vaguely aware of Lester Perkins skulking around behind him, watching as well. How much had he heard? Did the man have nothing better to do than be someone's shadow?

More important, what the hell did Sasha think she was doing with VanDerZanden? Flashing Nick an angry look over her shoulder, she nodded at the silver-haired high roller, then went off with him, easy as you please.

"Hey, boss, what's up?"

Ignoring Vito for a moment, Nick stared daggers at their backs, furious enough to kill....

"SO WHAT'S SO IMPORTANT that you had to talk to me tonight?" Sasha asked after Gaines handed her a roll of silver dollars and sat at the slot machine next to her. Though he eyed the rip in her knit dress where she'd freed herself from the moving bandwagon, he didn't comment. Popping his own roll open and pouring the silver dollars into a plastic cup, he asked, "Exactly how close have you gotten to Nick Donatelli?"

She did a double take and clenched the roll of coins. "That's none of your business."

"Anything to do with any Donatelli here in Las Vegas *is* my business."

Inserting three dollars, Gaines triggered the one-arm bandit. While the wheels of the slot machine were spinning, he reached into an interior jacket pocket and pulled out what looked like a leather billfold. No match on the slots. He glanced around as if to make certain no one was watching, then covertly flipped the leather open in such a way that even the casino cameras couldn't pick up his action.

Sasha's eyes widened as they lit on the shield inside. "You're—?"

"On the job." He slipped the shield back into his pocket. In a low tone, he told her, "The Donatellis are under official investigation by the federal government."

Which blew her mind. Here she had him pegged as a suspect—a possible prospective bridegroom, for Pete's sake—and he was one of the good guys.

"But Salvatore Donatelli went straight," she said, even remembering the *mostly* in Sally's reference to his participating in legal activities.

"Maybe he did. Maybe he didn't." Gaines inserted another three dollars. "But we can't overlook the fact that Glory Hale died in the same manner as Donatelli's former fiancée. You do know about the murders?"

Going even colder inside, she nodded. "So what do you want from me?"

"Your cooperation."

"You want me to spy on Nicky?"

Hardly an easy task, considering she'd just kissed him off royally.

"I'm not asking you to do any digging," Gaines said, feeding the machine as fast as it took his money. "Just keep your eyes open and let me know about anything out of the ordinary. And for the moment, play your slot machine so you don't raise anyone's suspicions."

Staring down at the unopened roll in her hand, she asked, "How do you know I won't go straight to Nicky and tell him about our conversation?"

"Because I've had you checked out. You care about your old friend JoJo Weston enough to try to find her. I believe that's why you got yourself tangled up with a man like Donatelli in the first place."

Amazed that she'd been the object of such close official scrutiny without ever realizing it, Sasha clenched her jaw. "Did you have anything to do with JoJo's disappearance?"

"Not a thing."

"But you haven't done anything to figure out what happened to her, either, have you?" He didn't answer, so Sasha pressed him. "You talked to JoJo like you're doing with me now, didn't you?" Wondering where a prospective groom fit into the picture, she said, "You got her to help you, maybe even pushed her straight into whatever trouble she's in!"

"Now, now, you can't blame the government here. Miss Weston never even agreed to do anything for us. She said she had to think about it first."

"That's exactly what *I* need to do." Sasha stood and slammed the roll of silver dollars on the table holding the slot machines. "Think about it, that is."

"Don't take too long," Gaines warned her. "Things seem to be heating up fast."

Wondering if he was referring to things between her and Nick or to the immediate danger of the situation she was in—no doubt he knew about the attempts on her life—Sasha turned her back on Gaines. Subtly aware of Nick still standing outside the showroom, following her every movement, she rushed across the casino, trying to block out his presence, as well as the bizarre musical cadence created by the slot machines.

She was starting to hear the damned sounds in her sleep!

Sasha raced past the blackjack tables without spotting Mac Schneider. She had no particular plan in mind, other than to get home as quickly as possible. So she made her way toward her rental car in the parking lot. And was frustrated when the thing wouldn't start. She slapped the flat of her hand against the steering wheel and willed herself not to cry. A dead battery wasn't the worst thing in the world that could happen to her.

But why wouldn't the car start? Her quickly aroused suspicions were assuaged when she realized the lights had been left on. She didn't remember having turned them on, but she must have done so without thinking.

Inside the Caribbean again, she called the rental company and got only an answering machine. She left a message and slammed the receiver down. Great. No car till morning. A taxi would have to do.

But once out on the street, she had little luck. The doorman had disappeared for the moment, and flagging a cab herself proved to be an exercise in futility. Several whizzed on by her. Finally one pulled up to the curb. She was relieved for the moment... until three drunk men pushed her out of the way.

"Hey, you ever heard of good manners?" Sasha yelled, her frustration rising to the boiling point.

The men ignored her. The taxi sped away. And when she glanced behind her through the glass doors, she spotted Nick, shouldering his way through the casino toward the very entrance where she stood. Was he coming this way because he'd seen her?

Whether or not he had, she was in no mood for another confrontation. Her emotions riding high, Sasha decided a walk to JoJo's complex would do her good. Hurrying south, she took an incisive look around the Strip, which had lost its innocent sense of fun for her in only five short days. She noticed the plastic beneath all the glittery bright lights, the drunk tourists weaving from one casino to the other to surrender their savings, not to mention the sleazy young men handing out brochures advertising houses of ill repute located outside the county.

Las Vegas. A neon harlot.

Shouldering her bag, she thought about her options. Work with the authorities. Tell Nick about Gaine's proposal. Leave. No, she couldn't do that. Not with JoJo still missing. Besides, the thought of leaving now—not ever seeing Nick again—brought a lump to her throat the size of the Big Apple.

After checking it out to make sure the shortcut looked safe, she turned at the Wild West construction site. A billboard announced the imminent reopening of the hotel-casino, but the renovation was still separated from the building on her left by chain link fencing, boards and scattered work lights.

Halfway across, she became aware of another presence when a scuffle echoed through the desolate urban canyon, its source behind her. Heart lurching, she glanced over her shoulder, noted a shadowy figure a distance behind her. The figure was running her way.

Twice, in less than twenty-four hours, someone had tried to kill her. In a town like Las Vegas, where the odds were against her, three times certainly would be the charm. She wasn't about to wait and see if this might be just another worker taking the shortcut. Since no one was around to hear her if she screamed, Sasha ran for all she was worth.

Behind her, leather slapped pavement, the accelerating sound echoing along the buildings and drumming through her ears. Desperate to find a hiding place, she looked to the construction site and was elated when she spotted a break in the chain link fencing.

She squeezed through and headed for the half-built parking structure. Materials lay in piles around the perimeter, as did heavy construction machinery. She stopped a moment to make up her mind... and heard him coming. At least she assumed the person chasing her was a *he*. Rather than running into an open area, where she would definitely be vulnerable, Sasha sneaked into a doorless cab attached to a crane and slipped behind the operator's seat.

Just in time.

The slap-slapping was now echoing around her.

Chapter Twelve

Curled as deep back into the cab as she could get, Sasha ducked her head into the shadows and held her breath. Heart thundering so hard she could hardly hear, she somehow became aware of the person directly outside. Who?

Even though she'd gotten a mere glance at the shadowy figure, she knew the person hadn't been a woman. Not Barbie or Caroline. Men ran more aggressively...and the silhouette had been bigger. But exactly how big?

Vito Tolentino big?

Or Gaines VanDerZanden big?

Maybe Gaines wasn't a federal agent, after all. Maybe he'd schmoozed her with a load of bunk and was really an enemy of the Donatelli family trying to even some old score. And maybe now he was after her because she hadn't agreed to his con.

Sasha didn't want to think it might be Nick.

Mouth dry, sick at heart, she considered the possibility, anyway.

Two women he'd been involved with had died after breaking up with him, the last one only a few months before and in this very same spot.

The realization that she fit the pattern—that she'd just broken up with Nick, as well—sent a creepy sensation crawling up her spine. Twice in twenty-four hours her life had been in jeopardy, and twice Nick had been Johnny-on-the-spot to rescue her. But that didn't mean Nick was guilty, Sasha told herself.

Only she wished she were a bigger believer in coincidence.

From the open doorway came the sound of feet shuffling over the gravel, as if the hunter were pacing restlessly, trying to get a fix on her direction. A low male curse was followed by a jarring *bam!* as a fist contacted the side of the cab, making her head pop away from its resting place.

Terror-stricken by the possibility of discovery, Sasha pressed a fist to her mouth so as not to scream. She'd survived one brutal face-to-face attack with a man out of control. She couldn't count on being able to survive another—couldn't count on being able to use what she'd learned in the Street Smarts Survival program. Practice was one thing. This was reality.

Grim reality.

Sweat trickled down her back and through the hollow between her breasts. The sweat of fear. Of not knowing. Of waiting. She was drenched in it.

Her stalker moved past the cab. Twisted like a pretzel, she dared not move. She glimpsed first a shadow, then a white trouser leg through the open doorway. The shadow kept going. The footsteps fading into the night.

Now the waiting began. Waiting to hear the renewed crunch of gravel. Waiting for his return. Minutes passed. Parts of an hour. More. Sasha waited so long, her limbs sailed past tingling straight to dead. She feared she could not get to her feet if she tried.

But should she?

She had to leave the safety of her hiding place sometime. But to go where? JoJo's apartment was out. He could be waiting for her there.

He. Whoever he was.

She didn't want to name him. Didn't want to name the man who'd somehow made her fall head-over-heels for him in less than a week's time.

Love. She put a name to her feelings for Nick. She didn't want to love him, but there it was. Had Mia loved him? And what about Glory? Had Nick played sick games with them—creating *accidents* from which he'd saved them—and then had he cornered them until they broke off their relationships with him? As the spurned lover, had he made their punishments *death?*

The man stalking her was wearing white trousers...like Nick.

She was going to be sick. But not in here, Sasha vowed. Outside. Her stomach was dropping fast. She had to get out of the cab.

Moving was difficult. Limbs screamed as blood rushed through them anew. And when she tried to rise, pain shot through her abused hip. She grunted, pulling her focus from the injury. Dancers often performed with painful injuries, and she was no exception. She could do this.

She stumbled out of the cab, chest heaving, sucking in the cool night air. Her stomach lurched a time or two...gave a warning tumble...then settled. She wouldn't be sick, after all.

Where to go?

The question plagued her as she moved off, eyes darting across every inch of the construction site.

He was gone. She could feel it. Relief shot through her.

Where to go?

The police. If she knew where to find them. She could return to the Strip and locate a pay phone, but that would be exposing herself. *He* might be there. Waiting. Nick. No, the Strip was no safer than JoJo's place.

Where to go?

Then it came to her. Mac Schneider had told her she should find him if she needed help. Protection from Nick. From the man she loved. Mac hadn't been at the blackjack tables. Undoubtedly his shift was over and he would be home. She hoped. The Groves—that was the name of his apartment complex. Only a few blocks from here.

Somehow, despite both the nerves and the pain that plagued her, she scudded along the construction site, then bravely put herself in the open the rest of the way, Sasha found herself safely in front of Mac's door a short while later. Apartment 4. She hit the doorbell and heard a faint buzz from the inside.

No answer. She tried again. Waited.

Sasha nearly broke down and cried when no response came. Throat choked with disappointment, she stood there, staring at the door as if her will could open it.

Now what?

She was still staring. Details came into focus. Like the fact that the door had a dead bolt, the same brand as the one used by the hotel.

The same brand as the key in her shoulder bag.

Adrenaline rushed through Sasha. It couldn't be. Still, she plunged her hand into her bag and found the metal length. Her hand shook as she guided it toward the lock.

She shook as the key turned easily.

The door opened. She stood staring. Waiting to regain her equilibrium. The key she'd found in JoJo's jewelry box fit Mac's door. Why would JoJo have Mac's key if they hadn't had a close relationship?

How close? Gonna-Get-Married-Chapel-of-Love close?

Taking a big breath, she stepped inside, shutting the door behind her.

The apartment was a lot like JoJo's in size and layout, but the furnishings were of better quality. More expensive. The television was the kind with a giant screen, hooked up to a costly stereo system. And the painting on the wall behind the couch and the sculpture on the fancy desk in the corner hadn't come cheap, either.

Something didn't sit right. Maybe a blackjack dealer made more money than a dancer—no doubt Mac got big tips from bettors on a hot streak. But why hide expensive furnishings in a low-rent complex?

Putting that question aside for the moment, she started her search for evidence that would link Mac and JoJo. Uncertain of what she might find, she chose to overlook nothing.

She started in the bedroom, with the closet and dresser drawers, but to her disappointment found no articles of clothing that might belong to her friend. No familiar contraceptives in the nightstand drawer, either.

In the bathroom, a single toothbrush denoted the apartment's lone occupant. As did the nearly empty medicine cabinet with its mouthwash and bottle of heavy-duty aspirin. Aspirin...her hip. Grabbing the bottle, she shook two free and took them with a handful of water.

In the kitchen, the refrigerator was nearly as bare as the cupboards. Some deli stuff, a few cans of beer and a bottle of wine.

She took a better look...a bottle of imported May wine.

JoJo's favorite.

With renewed hope that she was getting somewhere, Sasha set to the living room like a madwoman. She tore through magazines, checked the insides of the couches and chair for anything the furniture might have swallowed. But it wasn't until she set her shoulder bag down on the desk and riffled through the middle drawer that she found anything of interest.

Shoved in the back was a single sheet of fancy stationery. The paper had been handled so much it was worn.

A love letter?

But when Sasha unfolded the stationery, she deflated like a hot-air balloon. The handwriting was unfamiliar. Still, she gave the missive a glance...and then read in shock.

Dearest Marco,
I can hardly believe I went through with it. I got engaged to Nick like Papa said I should, and now Nick's refusing to cooperate. He's insisting on taking over Sally's affairs, and nothing I can say will budge him. I don't like all this arguing. It's like he knows. Nick says he loves me, but he scares me, Marco. I don't care what Papa says—I'm going to

break it off with him before something terrible happens.

Take care of yourself the best you can and write to me. I'll visit you soon, I promise, and bring you Mama's lemon sponge cake.

Love,
Mia

Mia? Sasha realized she was holding a letter written by Mia Scudella to her twin brother, Marco, who had been imprisoned at the time.

Here it was in black and white. The reason Mia had rejected Nick. Being engaged to Nick had been some kind of a trick to make him come to heel for Carmine Scudella. Only it hadn't worked. And Mia had been afraid. Afraid enough to break the engagement.

Sasha swallowed hard and the backs of her eyelids felt hot and scratchy.

Had Nick figured it all out and killed Mia out of revenge?

Mia. What in the world was Mac doing with a letter from Mia Scudella to her brother? Unless...

Marco Scudella...Mac Schneider.

The truth spiked her like the cool breeze wafting through the opened door. She whipped around, startled to be facing Mac, who was standing there, staring, his intense gaze focused on the letter in her hand.

"I never got the lemon sponge cake," he told her calmly. "Donatelli killed my sister before she could come visit me like she promised."

Realizing Mac was indeed Marco Scudella, a professional criminal, Sasha had a hard time breathing evenly and her pulse did a little dance. "Um, Mac, I can explain—"

The slamming door cut off any excuse she might come up with. "I'm a little surprised to find you in my apartment," he said. "Surprised, but not shocked. Not much has shocked me since my sister was brutally murdered by the man who'd professed to love her. I read that letter over and over. Hundreds of times. No, thousands. And I knew what I had to do."

Her mouth was going dry. She was in trouble and she knew it. "I take it Nicky doesn't know who you are."

"Not a clue. Though we grew up in the same town, we never associated as kids. And then I had some bad luck, was sentenced to a stretch in the pen. Which unfortunately got a little longer. Trouble with other inmates. That was before Donatelli got involved with his father's business. Before he got engaged to my sister."

"Who went after Nicky on your father's orders," Sasha reminded him, remembering. "Sally said they got engaged despite Carmine Scudella's objections."

Mac grinned. "My father knows how to manipulate people."

"A family trait." Like father like daughter like son. "So what are you after?" she asked, setting the letter on the desk.

"Revenge." His mouth drew into a bitter line and set an unattractive edge to his features. "That bastard murdered my sister and he wasn't even arrested."

"He did have an alibi." Sasha was reminding herself, as well as him.

He laughed. "I know all about alibis."

Which made her wonder what crimes Mac *hadn't* served time for. "So you're what...planning on killing Nicky?"

"Eventually. After I bleed him dry. Destroy him financially. Money meant more to him than Mia, so I figure that's where he'll hurt the most." Mac moved closer to her. "I've been looking for a way to get him good since I started working for him a couple months ago. I finally found one." Now he seemed to be hashing over his grievances to himself. "If only JoJo had left well enough alone. But she had to find the damn comb right after I got my hands on it. She put it someplace safe, she said, until she could give it back to the bastard."

Sasha's antennae went up. "Caroline's comb?" Why in the world was it so important? "The one with the missing emerald?"

"The emerald's not really missing. The police have it," Mac informed her. "They found it in her apartment, and while that wasn't actually the murder scene, they're keeping it as evidence."

This wasn't making sense. Frowning, she said, "Caroline lost that comb arguing with Mia?" Then how had JoJo gotten her hands on it twelve years later?

"Not Mia . . . Glory. I figure Caroline went to face down Glory about her brother. She's very possessive." He laughed. "But you probably already know that."

Silence stretched between them for a moment. Sasha was getting an uneasy feeling. "So you believe Nicky killed Glory, too, right?"

"Nah." His eyes glittered as they fixed on her. "Glory was a snoop, like you. She figured out who I was, what I was up to. She would have told."

Sasha stared. Her pulse drummed through her veins and she licked lips that had suddenly gone dry. Not only had the charming blackjack dealer turned out to be a hardened criminal, but he was a murderer, as well. She knew it would be a miracle if she got away from Mac alive. He would have to kill her so she couldn't tell.

Rather, he would try. She was trained to fight back, Sasha reminded herself.

She would get away...somehow.

"I had to kill Glory," Mac went on in a conversational tone, as if he were speaking of an everyday event. "Donatelli thought it was his sister, though. Because of the comb. He was keeping it from the police, trying to protect her. JoJo told me all about it. We didn't keep secrets." He laughed again, his face suddenly appearing evil. "Well, JoJo didn't, anyway. I got into Donatelli's apartment and cracked his wall safe and took the comb." He *tch-tched* to himself. "Such an obvious place. Donatelli would have given up a lot to get the damn comb back, to protect his sister. But JoJo spoiled that for me."

Things were starting to come into focus for Sasha, the most important fact being that Nick hadn't killed Glory. And if he hadn't killed Glory, maybe he hadn't killed Mia, either.

Hope lightened her heart a bit.

"So you purposely killed Glory Hale in the same way your sister was killed...by stabbing her through the heart. You were trying to make Nicky look guilty."

"I figured the police couldn't ignore two murders that were so much alike. Both women rejected Donatelli. Both killed in the same manner. But, again, the authorities gave the bastard a pass."

"What did you do with JoJo?" Sasha asked. If she could get out of the apartment alive, she could rescue her friend.

"I don't know what happened to that whining little...if only I could get my hands on her."

Sasha gauged the distance to the door. About a dozen feet. "So you were the one she was going to marry," she said, pretty certain she could make it to the door.

"A temporary price I was willing to pay so that she could hand Donatelli over to me on a silver platter. They were good friends. He talked to her. And she foolishly told me everything. Even finding the comb here didn't clue her in." Again, his expression darkened. "But someone warned her off at the last minute and she did a vanishing act."

And Sasha knew that if he found JoJo, he wouldn't allow her friend to live, either.

He added, "And then *you* showed up and started digging where you didn't belong."

"So you decided to drown me in the swimmer's tank." Elated that Nick hadn't been playing sick games with her, after all, she covertly slipped her hand back through the strap of her shoulder bag on the desk. "And when that didn't work, you tried to flatten me on the bandwagon."

"Must have been Donatelli, 'cause it wasn't me," Mac insisted.

He was trying to fool her, Sasha thought, to get her off guard. She wouldn't believe him. "I suppose you didn't chase me through the construction site earlier tonight, either." She focused on his smug expression. Got ready to run.

"Return to the scene of the crime? Not hardly. I haven't had any reason to do anything to hurt you...until now." With that, Mac plunged his hand into his pocket as if reaching for a weapon.

Before he could complete the action, she swung out and smacked him hard, square in the face, with her loaded shoulder bag. Then, backed by his shout of fury, she flew to the door, opened it and ran for all she was worth. Instinct turned her in the direction of JoJo's apartment complex and fear lent speed to her feet.

Mac wasn't far behind her, but he didn't have the physical training she did as a dancer. Adrenaline and those aspirins she'd taken in his apartment kept her bruised hip from slowing her. One block. Two. Mac stayed right behind her, unable to close the gap.

Sasha prayed for an audience, but no one was listening. No cars. No pedestrians. Anyone not working the Strip was probably tucked neatly into bed. She was on her own. She didn't even know how she could get into JoJo's apartment—the key was in her shoulder bag back in Mac's place.

She crossed the parking lot toward JoJo's building anyway. At least she was familiar with the layout. She was nearing the swimming pool when a shout came from what sounded like a good distance behind her.

"Sasha!"

The sound of Nick's voice took her off her stride. She hesitated...and was tackled. With Mac's weight on her, she hit the ground hard. Felt the air whoosh out of her. He rolled away from the pool, jumped to his feet and pulled something from his pocket. With a click, a knife blade appeared.

"Three's the charm," Mac puffed. "Now the police will have to arrest Donatelli!"

She was ready...on her butt, resting her weight on her hands behind her, legs toward Mac. A man's strength was in his arms, a woman's in her legs. And she was a dancer, which made her legs a double threat. He lunged toward her, and she kicked out, aiming low. Her foot glanced off his groin. Not a solid hit, but enough to slow him down.

"Son of a bitch!"

He came at her again, but she kept him at bay with her legs raised, her feet flashing. Her heel made contact with his shin. He swore viciously. No matter which way he feinted, she spun on her rear, ready to kick.

Then, his expression maniacal, Mac threw himself at her, knife hand swinging. She kicked out at the weapon but his arm swept out of the way...then returned before she could recoup. A searing pain ripped along her thigh. She screamed. And struck out again with the bleeding leg.

Contact.

She heard Mac's knee break.

His knife went skittering just past her head, while he went down with a yowl.

Another, "Sasha!" This one closer. "Hang on."

With Nick distracting her, Mac gained the advantage. He got past her guard and the next thing she knew, he was on top of her, straddling her, reaching for the knife. Sasha pounded at him, but he had one hand around her throat. He was squeezing. Cutting off her air. Black spots danced before her eyes. She dug her nails into the flesh of his hand, and when his fingers flexed, she grabbed onto them and twisted, feeling one pop out of the joint.

"Ah-h-h!"

But he had the knife in his good hand. It rose in an arc. The blade was descending...

And then not.

Suddenly Mac was lifted off her, limbs flailing like a puppet. The knife flew into the swimming pool with a splash. Nick held him in the air, shaking him until Mac smacked him in the face with an elbow. Freed, Mac crashed to the ground and came up on his good leg, his shoulder jarring Nick square in the solar plexus.

They went flying, rolling over the ground, punching at one another, the sound of flesh hitting flesh punctuated with grunts. Having caught her breath, Sasha got to her feet. The two men were rising, also, Mac looking the worse for wear.

Behind her, the wail of a siren split the night. Alerted, Mac hopped on his one good leg as if he could make a run for it.

"Give it up, Schneider," Nick said, hauling off and making contact one more time. His human punching bag teetered and fell into the pool. As uniformed cops raced toward them, guns drawn, he turned to her. "You all right?"

She nodded and—forcing to the back of her mind Mac's insistence that Nick was the one who'd been trying to kill her—flew into Nick's arms. After all, he hadn't had anything to do with this incident. Mac had been about to knife her like he had Glory when Nick had come to her rescue.

"All right, hands where we can see them!" a cop shouted as several men swarmed around them.

"Nicky...one thing," she said. He had a right to know before anyone else. "The man in the swimming pool...his name's not Schneider. It's Marco Scudella."

Chapter Thirteen

Marco Scudella.

More than an hour later, after having gone to the police station, where he'd given his statement about arriving in Sasha's parking lot in time to see the creep go after her, Nick couldn't get over his shock.

How could he have been so stupid as to employ Mia's twin and not know it?

He hadn't ever really known Marco, though. And twelve years seemed like forever. He wasn't even certain he would recognize Mia herself should she come back from the dead.

"Don't worry, Miss Brozynski," the detective in charge was saying. "We'll put out an all points bulletin about JoJo Weston. We'll find her."

"Great, you finally believe me," Sasha said.

To Nick's ears, she sounded despondent. He also wondered why she hadn't told the authorities about her dip in the tank and the incident on the bandwagon. Not that he was going to press his luck....

"Are you sure you don't want a ride to an emergency room?" the detective asked again, indicating her cut leg.

"It's just a scratch," she insisted. "Some more peroxide will do the trick."

Upon arriving at the station, she'd used their first-aid kit to clean out and bandage the shallow wound.

"I'll see that she's taken care of," Nick said, rising abruptly.

Sasha stood, too, but gave him a sideways glance that made his skin crawl. What was wrong with her now?

"Here, don't forget your purse," the detective said, handing it to her.

One of the uniforms, who'd been securing Scudella's place until the search warrant arrived, had brought the leather bag back to the station. Now she took it gratefully, clinging to the strap like a lifeline.

Nick wanted to be Sasha's lifeline in the worst way. He wanted her to come into his arms willingly, as she had earlier. But something between them had changed in the short time it had taken them to get to the station. It was almost as if he could hear the wheels of her mind turning...speculating...about him. And undoubtedly she was still angry about their fight earlier. He shouldn't have asked her to swear that she was telling him the truth.

Trust went two ways. He was just so used to seeing the worst side of people that he had difficulty trusting anyone—especially women he got involved with.

Grimly, he led her from the police station, noticing that she was limping slightly.

"Maybe you should let a doctor look you over."

"No doctor," she insisted, clinging to that damned shoulder bag, probably so she wouldn't have to touch him. "I'll be all right."

"You don't need help from anyone, huh?" he asked, thinking about how close that knife had come.

"I didn't say that." She sounded indignant when she did say, "But for your information, Mac wouldn't have gotten the jump on me if you hadn't distracted me by calling out."

"My apologies for caring what happened to you."

"Listen, I'm sorry." She rubbed at her shoulder. "I'm not at my best right now."

Was she really sorry? She was tight as a bowstring. Ready to pop. Why? The police had Marco Scudella where he belonged. The only other thing that could be bothering her was . . . him. She was *still* angry.

So why had she thrown herself into his arms? Gratitude? He'd been hoping it was because she cared.

"C'mon. I'll give you a ride home." He indicated his car a few yards away.

She stopped, looking torn. She just stood there, not saying anything. It was up to him.

"I'm sorry for before, okay?" An awkward apology, but he wasn't used to asking anyone to forgive his actions.

"It's not that . . . exactly."

"Well, then what is it, exactly?"

"I didn't tell the police everything." She sounded as if she might regret the fact. "Mac . . . Marco . . . denied trying to hurt me before. The tank . . . the bandwagon . . . the construction site."

Construction site.

"What are you trying to say, Sasha?"

"Not a whole lot of people would have reason to want to see me hurt."

"But I do?"

She bit her lip, then said, "The comb...Marco said you were protecting Caroline. Exactly how far would you go to protect her?"

His blood went cold at what was tantamount to an accusation. One he refused to answer. "You knew about the comb, and yet you didn't say a word to the cops."

"Tell me about it, Nick." Her expression was stricken and she seemed barely able to hold herself together. "Marco broke into your safe for the comb. Then JoJo found it, and suspecting what he was up to, she took it. She was going to give it back to you. So what was the whole story?"

He supposed he could assuage her suspicions, especially now that it was clear that Marco killed the show girl.

"When Glory's body was found, the police came straight to the Caribbean to tell me about it. While they were questioning me, Vito slipped out and got to her place before they did. He was looking for anything of mine that might incriminate me. He found the comb and knew it was Caroline's. Only he didn't realize the stone was missing."

"So he brought the comb to you," Sasha said, "and you thought your sister might be guilty."

"I faced Caroline down. She swore she didn't do it—that she'd merely had an argument with Glory over me—and I believed her."

"Then why keep the comb from the police?"

"*I* believed her; they might not have."

"So you did it to protect your sister." Sasha gave him a strange look filled with foreboding. "And what about

Mia's murder—did you ask her about that one, too? Or did you have to?''

The silence between them grew thick. Finally, Nick asked through gritted teeth, ''And what do you think?''

''I don't know, Nicky. Marco killed Glory in his insane quest for revenge against you because he thought you killed his sister.''

Nick clenched his jaw and asked, ''Was anything between us real? Or were you just using me to find JoJo?'' He saw the truth written across her lovely face. *Guilt.* ''I called you on it up front,'' he said, remembering the scene in the elevator. ''I thought that cleared the air. But you were never sure of me, were you?''

''No.''

Anger growing, he asked, ''So you did what? Purposely made me fall for you so you could get to me where I lived?''

''I, uh...'' Her throat worked, but she couldn't deny it.

Another mistake. He'd fallen for Sasha even harder than he had for Mia. More angry with her than he'd been even with his first love, Nick turned his back on Sasha and stalked to his car before he could do something he would regret.

Fury making him see red, he zoomed off into the night without looking back.

DEPRESSED, LET DOWN, filled with unshed tears for something that was never meant to be, Sasha wandered off blindly.

Nick had wanted her to reassure him that she cared, that she didn't blame him for anything, and she hadn't been able to do so. What was wrong with her? Deep down in her heart, how could she really believe he was capable of murder when he'd saved her bacon over and over again.

He wouldn't have been so hurt and angry if he'd been the one to put her in danger in the first place, she rationalized.

And yet . . . he hadn't given her any reassurances.

She knew that Mac-Marco had killed Glory. She also knew that he hadn't killed Mia. And Nick hadn't given her the satisfaction of a denial. He'd wanted to know if she believed him capable of murder.

Why couldn't he have said the words: *I didn't do it.*

Swallowing hard, she remembered he'd wanted her to swear that she hadn't been in with JoJo on some blackmail scheme. That had pushed her over the edge, had made her tell him off and walk out on him.

So why had she expected better of him?

But now, with time to think about it, she realized that while Nick's loyalty went unquestioned, that didn't make him a murderer. More likely Caroline was the guilty one. Or Vito. She hadn't given the security man enough thought, yet he was the one who'd had the guts to go into Glory's place to clean up for his boss *after* she was murdered . . . even with the police practically breathing down his neck.

And what about JoJo? Sasha didn't believe Nick had her friend. Mac certainly had wanted to get his hands on her, which meant he had nothing to do with her disappearance. Again, that left Caroline and Vito. But Caroline didn't seem an even match for an athletic dancer . . . so that made Vito more likely. Cleaning up after Nick again?

Not that Nick would want to believe it.

Although Sasha really hadn't been paying much attention to her wandering feet, she wasn't surprised when she found herself on the Strip, barely a block from the Caribbean. She had to find Nick, tell him she was sorry, clear the air between them and get him to help her find JoJo no matter what. Her friend's life was the important thing here.

She limped through the casino, her disheveled appearance turning a few heads. She ignored the stares and took the elevator up to the penthouse. But Nick wasn't there. Sasha returned to the main floor, looking everywhere for him. He wasn't in the casino, either. On the odd chance that he might have gone into the showroom, she decided to check it out.

Eyes boring into the showroom's shadows as she descended part of the way down the steps, she called out, "Nicky, you here?" But the place seemed deserted.

Dejected, she stared at the tank, then at the bandwagon, which was now level with the stage. Who had been responsible for her accidents and why? And what about JoJo's disappearance? There had to be a connection. If only JoJo had been able to say more when she'd called the other night...from Yale Riker's cellular phone...a phone that had been lost right here in the theater. Rather down amongst the sets and props....

A scuffling alerted Sasha to another presence. Heart slamming against her ribs, she whipped around. But it was only Lester Perkins standing at the top of the stairs. She sagged with relief.

"Hi, Lester."

As he drew closer, his homely face pulled into a frown and his glasses bobbled crookedly on his nose. "What happened to you?"

"I had a run-in with a blackjack dealer—Mac Schneider."

"He tried to hurt you, too?"

Wondering why the *too,* she told the maintenance man, "He tried to kill me. But he's behind bars now. And his real name is Marco Scudella."

"Scudella . . . no wonder."

Lester was obviously familiar with the name. As he should be. He'd worked for Sally Donatelli before he'd been convicted and served time. And then he'd worked for the crime boss via Carmine Scudella until Nick had taken over.

At the moment, Lester was looking a little freaked, so she asked, "What did you know about Mac?"

Avoiding her gaze, he said, "He wasn't a nice man, that's all." He continued down the stairs, away from her.

"No, there's more, isn't there?" Sasha pressed, following him despite her bone-deep exhaustion. "You know something."

Glancing over his shoulder at her, he punched at his glasses with a shaky hand. "Gotta go. . . ."

She hurried to play catch-up and grabbed his arm. "Don't. Please. What do you know about Mac?"

Lester shifted from one foot to the other, then blurted out, "He killed Glory Hale!"

Not exactly common knowledge. Even though the Caribbean was a small community, as Mac had said, this was too soon for word to have gotten around. But Lester *knew.* Only one way.

"You saw the murder?"

"I saw Mac leave the casino. He looked around, sneaky-like, thought no one was watching. But I saw him go after her. His face…it was real mean. Then the police came later, said she was dead."

"He did kill her," Sasha told him, wondering why Lester hadn't relayed this information to the cops. "He admitted it."

"I knew it!" He clambered onto the stage. "I knew I was right all along!"

He wasn't exactly making sense…or was he?

He tried to hurt you, too? echoed through her head.

And Lester's not having told the police…

Trying to keep her growing suspicion from her voice, Sasha asked, "Right about what, Lester?"

"About Miss Weston."

JoJo! A thrill shot along her nerves. And suddenly she knew. Still, she calmly asked, "What about her?"

Lester seemed to be trying to make up his mind. A curt nod and he said, "Come with me." He approached a trapdoor to stage left. "I got something to show you."

It suddenly hit Sasha that Lester wasn't wearing his usual turquoise maintenance uniform. Instead he was dressed in a white suit and tropical print shirt, the sort that Nick usually wore. The man who'd followed her onto the construction site had been wearing white trousers….

"Um, Lester? Where exactly are we going?"

He bristled and sounded quite unlike himself. "Do you wanna find your friend or not?"

Unable to resist the opportunity to find JoJo, Sasha followed, confident that Lester wouldn't get the upper hand this time. Why hadn't she seriously considered the maintenance man before? Always in the background, always drooling over show girls, always appearing and disappearing at will.

Lester Perkins knew the theater's secrets.

And now she knew his.

Had JoJo been right under her dancing toes all along? For Sasha was certain Lester had been keeping her friend here at the theater—where he came and went at will.

Tracking back through a props area, making certain Lester stayed in front of her where she could see him, Sasha asked, "You really like JoJo, don't you?"

"She likes me, too. That's why I have to protect her."

"From who?"

"Mac Schneider, for one," he said, as if there were others. "I saw how he looked at her...real angry, just like with Glory. Only JoJo was going to marry him. She didn't know."

"She's not in danger from Mac anymore, Lester. The police have him."

They'd gotten away from the area she was familiar with and were heading toward the back wall. Lester opened a door that led to another set of stairs heading downward. The maw waiting for them was dark and dank and spooky.

"I already lost Glory," he said. "I couldn't let the same thing happen to JoJo."

He talked about the women as if he'd had a real relationship with them. Sasha mulled this over as they descended to the subbasement. Lester thought he'd lost Glory and was worried enough about JoJo to keep her secreted from the world. What made him so attached to these particular women? The fact that they had been nice to him...or the fact that Nick Donatelli had dated them? Lester had asked her to go for a drink with him, right before her involuntary dip in the tank.

And now he was dressed just like Nick....

"Mr. D will be happy you're taking care of JoJo," she said, testing. When he didn't answer, she pursued it. "You will tell him, won't you?"

He stopped at the bottom of the stairs and looked up at her. "He won't care. He has you now."

"And you have JoJo." The woman Nick used to date. "What about Glory?"

"She liked me, too, but she died."

As had Mia Scudella.

The chain of thoughts leading to the ultimate conclusion took Sasha's very breath away.

As she followed Lester through a maze of dark corridors, brushing aside an occasional spiderweb, Sasha wondered if they'd be able to find their way out of there easily. She and JoJo. She *felt* her friend's presence. She would get JoJo to freedom, no matter if she had to hurt Lester—though loath to do it, she would if she had to. But first she wanted the whole truth.

"Lester, have you always liked Mr. D's women?"

"We have a connection, Mr. D and me. Have from the first."

Unbelievable. He identified with Nick. Closely enough to kill for him?

She forced out, "It must have hurt you when you found out what Mia Scudella did to Mr. D."

Lester stopped in front of a heavy wooden door built into ancient brick. "You should've stayed in New York," he said, his eyes glazed behind the thick glasses. "Everything would have been okay then."

Sasha's skin crawled, but she refused to quit before she got some answers. "Why should I have stayed in New York? Lester, why did you try to kill me?"

"Kill you?" He shook his head so hard his glasses went crooked in the other direction. "No, I never did."

"What about the tank?" she pressed. "The bandwagon. The construction site."

"I was only trying to scare you, to make you go away."

"You did a hell of a job." *Spooky bastard!*

He opened the door. Sasha's pulse raced as she half glanced inside the dimly lit room, barren and depressing, without taking her attention completely from Lester. On the cot against the wall lay a still form huddled beneath a blanket.

Her heart lurched, pounded crazily.

"I was trying to make you leave us alone, is all," he was saying.

"JoJo?" Hope rising, Sasha asked Lester, "Is she all right?"

As if he didn't hear the question, he went on, "I was gonna make you go back to New York because you were gonna take JoJo away from me. I can't let you do that."

Recognizing the threat in his voice, she gathered herself together, ready for what might possibly be the fight of her life. But when she heard a familiar voice call, "Sasha, is that really you?" and then saw a bright red head pop free of the covers, she was momentarily distracted.

The split second was all Lester needed. Pain and a cascade of lights exploded in her head ... and then the lights went out.

"Nicky," Sasha mumbled as she struggled back to consciousness through a haze of pain.

"So it's Nicky, is it?" came a familiar voice, both worried and amused.

Feeling as if her head were larger than the rest of her, Sasha groaned and opened her eyes to see JoJo staring down at her, smiling through her tears. "What happened?"

"Lester bopped you one." Bending over her, JoJo swiped at a wet cheek, wiping away the proof that she'd been crying. "Thank God he didn't kill you."

"Oh, JoJo, thank God *you're* all right!" Sasha said, forcing herself into a sitting position.

Other than appearing stressed, JoJo was a beautiful sight for sore eyes. Sasha's eyes were actually tearing, too—whether from the pain in her skull or from the joy of seeing her friend at last, she wasn't certain. Perhaps both. She threw her arms around JoJo, and the two women hugged for all they were worth.

"Oh, JoJo, you don't know what I've been through trying to find you."

Sniffling, JoJo clung to her. "I figured you must have been going nuts when I didn't show at the wedding chapel."

"At least I knew you were alive when you called." Sasha looked around the dump that seemed to be an old janitor's closet. No phone here. She pulled free of JoJo's hug. "How did you manage it, anyway?"

"I begged Lester to let me take a shower, convinced him that since no one was around, no one would ever know. Here, let me help you up."

With JoJo to steady her, Sasha got to her feet. A slight wooziness passed in seconds. Her friend led her to a chair, then looked into her eyes.

"No concussion as far as I can tell. Not that I'm an expert. But that leg..." JoJo grimaced. "What happened?"

"Sit and stop fussing," Sasha told her, determined to get JoJo's story first. And when JoJo perched on the bed opposite, Sasha went back to the night of the phone call. "So Lester took you up to the women's dressing room?"

"That's what I was hoping for. I figured I'd be able to get away from him somehow. But he took me to this old extra dressing room right above here in the first basement. On the way, I spotted a cellular phone someone had left among the props. I filched it when Lester wasn't looking."

"Yale left his phone down there. Go on."

"I thought Lester'd give me some privacy, so I called from the shower room...but of course he caught me." JoJo heaved a big sigh. "Now he's caught you, as well."

"We'll get out of here," Sasha said with confidence, despite feeling as if she'd been trampled by a herd of wild horses.

"You think I haven't been trying?"

"But there's two of us now. We can overpower him."

"I sure hope so. I've forgotten what daylight and fresh air are like."

"How did Lester manage to lock you up down here in the first place?"

"I made the mistake of telling him about the wedding. Said he had a present for me and Mac, and that he was keeping it down here. Like a fool, I trusted him, followed him. Then he gave me some bunk about Mac not being the man I thought he was, and that he had to keep me here for my own safety. Lester Perkins is out of his mind. He thinks that Mac was the one who murdered Glory...uh, she was another show girl.''

Sasha's turn to grimace. ''I know all about it.'' She figured that if part of JoJo hadn't believed Lester, she would have called the man she loved, rather than her ex-roomie, to come to her rescue. ''And JoJo...Mac did murder her. He tried killing me tonight.''

JoJo stifled her cry of distress behind a shaky hand. Her gaze lowered to the cut scarring Sasha's leg, then raised to meet her friend's. ''Why?'' she asked so softly Sasha sensed the question rather than heard it. ''Because I found out who he really was.'' No easy way to do this, Sasha blurted, ''Marco Scudella.''

JoJo's mouth gaped.

For the next quarter of an hour, Sasha gave her an edited rundown of what had happened since her arrival in Las Vegas, skipping any details not pertinent to the crimes committed. Skipping what had happened between her and Nick especially. When she finished, JoJo was ashen, despondent, silent tears streaming down her cheeks.

Sasha touched her hand. ''I'm sorry.''

''And I'm stupid.'' JoJo laughed, but didn't stop crying.

Making Sasha's heart break for her. ''You're not stupid, you just fell in love.''

JoJo shook her head. ''All that secrecy Mac insisted on, saying it would be more fun to keep our wedding a surprise...and then his pumping me for information about Nick.''

"How did he explain that?"

"He didn't. I thought he was jealous because he'd seen me having a drink with Nick after we'd started dating. Actually, I was just reassuring Nick about his protecting Caroline—he believed she was innocent. Anyway, Mac got me to talk. I knew something was wrong when I found the comb. I tried to tell myself Mac stole it out of his crazy jealousy. I meant to return the comb to Nick and marry Mac as planned. Damn. Could I have been a bigger fool?"

"Hey, love is hard on all of us."

Red-eyed, JoJo sniffled and blinked at her. "Nicky? You did call him Nicky when you were coming to. Have you perhaps left out a detail or two?"

Sasha shifted uncomfortably. "Uh, maybe a few things. I didn't realize you and Nicky...uh, Nick...had something going."

"What?" Seeming genuinely amused, JoJo chuckled. "Nick Donatelli and I were only seeing each other as friends. Jeez, Sasha, you oughta know my type by now. I mean Nick's okay in the looks department, and he can be really nice when he tries—"

"Enough," Sasha said, grinning and feeling inordinately relieved considering their situation. "I should have known. We've never been attracted to the same man before. Plus, Nicky said he'd never slept with you, though I didn't know whether or not to believe it."

"Believe it." JoJo sobered. "Mac was the first man who got to me in a long, long time."

As Nick had been for her. JoJo's love life was down the toilet, and Sasha wondered if she hadn't flushed hers, as well.

"Why couldn't I have told Nicky I believed in him?" she murmured. "He went away thinking I suspected him of murdering Mia. I just couldn't make myself trust him."

"And the trust thing wouldn't have anything to do with the attack last year, right?"

The aftermath of which had been rough on her emotions and dealings with men, as JoJo well knew. JoJo had been there for her, Sasha thought, through the recuperation of her body and at least the partial mending of her spirit. Depressed that she hadn't done as well by her friend and managed JoJo's release, Sasha moved to the bed and wrapped an arm around her shoulders.

"You're a wise woman, JoJo. Now if only you could see into the future, tell me that all is not lost."

"All is not lost. At least you'll get the chance to make things right," JoJo assured her with a sad little smile. "If we ever get out of here."

"Teamwork. That's what it'll take. We'll work on a plan together."

At least to set them free.

Nick was another story.

Sasha wouldn't blame him if he never forgave her, even if she swore she didn't believe he killed Mia.

Question was, who did?

BY THE TIME NICK pulled up to the Caribbean and gave his keys to one of the car jockeys, all the anger was drained from him. Now all that was left was worry. He'd stopped by JoJo's apartment to make sure Sasha was all right, but she'd never arrived home. Since she'd been in town for such a short time, he could only think of one other place he might find her.

Here, at his hotel, waiting for another showdown.

Despite the fact that dawn would be arriving soon and the casino was nearly empty, Vito was on the floor, pacing as if something were bugging him.

"Boss, I was waiting for you. I heard rumors about Mac Schneider really being—"

"Marco Scudella," Nick confirmed. "Not only that, he's the one who killed Glory."

Vito let out a big breath. "That lets Caroline off the hook."

"Yeah."

At least where Glory Hale was concerned. He wasn't certain about Mia Scudella. For twelve years he hadn't had a clue to his ex-fiancé's murderer. Then, when Vito found Caroline's comb at Glory's place, he'd wondered if his sister hadn't been responsible for both deaths. She'd said not, and most of him had believed her.

Most of him had believed that Vito was innocent, too. The man who'd been like a second father to him had supplied him with both of his alibis.

Only trouble was, Nick hadn't been with Vito during either murder.

Knowing that Vito had done many questionable things for his father from the time Sally had saved him from the gutter, Nick hadn't looked too closely at Vito's motives for lying. He'd wanted to believe the big man he loved had his best interests at heart and had been preventing Nick from being railroaded for crimes he hadn't committed.

"Seems we were wrong about JoJo," Nick told Vito. "She didn't steal the comb. Mac did. JoJo took it from him, planned on returning it. So JoJo's in trouble,

Vito." He scrutinized the older man. "Mac was the intended groom. Someone has her, but he denies it was him. You don't have any thoughts, do you?"

Stiffening, Vito stared at him as if he knew what Nick was asking him. "Yeah, I got thoughts."

But he didn't confirm or deny his knowing anything about JoJo's disappearance, just as he'd never confirmed or denied knowing anything about Mia's murder. Nick had to take him on faith, no matter how hard that might be.

Doing his best, he nodded. "You haven't seen Sasha in the last hour, have you?"

The big man relaxed. "I only got back to the floor about ten minutes ago. I had a late supper."

"Thanks. If you see her, don't let her get away."

Not before he could tell her a few things, including the fact that he was crazy about her. More in love than he'd ever been with Mia. Even before he'd figured out Mia was conning him for her father, he'd known she was selfish and self-centered. Sasha was selfless. She'd nearly gotten herself killed trying to find her best friend, but danger hadn't deterred her.

She was the kind of woman he'd been waiting for all his life, and she didn't even know it.

Rather than taking the elevator up to his penthouse, he went instead to the showroom, half expecting to find Sasha waiting for him there. The big room was empty. His footsteps echoed on the steps. Halfway to the floor, he stopped and stared at the stage, trying to conjure up Sasha by sheer will alone.

He heard someone moving around. His heart picked up a beat. "Sasha?"

"Just me, Mr. D." Lester popped free of a trap on the stage. "Haven't seen Miss Brozynski since after the show."

"Thanks, Lester."

Something about the maintenance man caught Nick for a moment. Lester seemed nervous. Anxious. What the hell was he doing in the theater at this time of night? Nick wondered. And what had he been doing in one of the basements?

Waving as if saying *good-night,* Nick backed off, left the showroom. But he didn't go far. He waited in the shadows until Lester, furtively glancing around, left. He got a good look at the white suit and flower-printed shirt similar to his own. When he was certain the maintenance man was on his way out, Nick returned to the showroom.

He took the stairs two at a time.

Tap-tap-tap-tap-tap... tap-tap.

His pulse drummed when he heard the familiar cadence. The way JoJo used to tap at his door to let him know she was there—some old joke between her and Sasha because of a pesty admirer. Sasha had heard it, too, just before being taken for a ride on the bandwagon. He descended to the basement through a trapdoor, relieved that Lester hadn't turned off the safety lights. Had the maintenance man been chasing down the source of the sound, or had he known where it had come from?

Tap-tap-tap-tap-tap... tap-tap.

Nick followed the metallic ring to an area of the basement he didn't know too well. He waited to hear the tapping again, and then determined it might be coming from below. He found the stairs.

The maze of corridors in the subbasement was unfamiliar to him, but he concentrated on the rhythm that sounded as if someone were drumming on the plumbing. Someone. JoJo?

Tap-tap-tap-tap-tap . . . tap-tap.

He followed the sound to what he thought was its source—a bolted door. Quickly, he slid both bolts back and swung open the wooden panel to face blackness.

Boldly stepping inside anyway, he called out, "JoJo?" just before something heavy crashed down and splintered across his back and head.

Chapter Fourteen

"We got him! Turn on the light!" Sasha shouted, still gripping the chair in both hands.

The pitiful, bare bulb blinked on. Her elation quickly turned to dismay. Not Lester, after all.

"My God, it's Nicky!" Dropping what was left of the decrepit wooden chair that had too easily splintered, she got down on her knees and turned him over on his back. "Nicky, say something."

Groaning, Nick managed to open his eyes. "Anyone ever tell you you're a dangerous woman, Sasha Brozynski?"

"She's been told," JoJo stated. "Hey, Nick, thanks for coming to the rescue."

"JoJo, that you?"

"In the flesh."

Nick winced and tried to sit up.

Sasha flattened a hand against his chest and kept him where he was. "Hey, stay there for a minute until you get your breath." She had a few things to say to him and wondered if she should do it now, with JoJo there.

Before she had a chance to open her mouth, a petulant voice came from behind her. "You ruined it!"

Sasha whipped around as Lester Perkins grabbed her arm and jerked her to her feet. Her eyes widened when they met the knife in his other hand, mere inches from her throat. Her mouth went dry and she had difficulty swallowing. Everything she'd learned in her Street Smarts Survival program flew right out of her head.

"Lester!" JoJo cried. "Please put the knife down before you accidentally hurt my friend."

But Lester ignored JoJo. His entire being was focused on Sasha. "It's all your fault. If you hadn't of been snooping around, no one would ever know. Then everything would'a been all right."

"I won't press charges," JoJo said calmly. "I promise."

"Liar! You're all liars!" Spittle sprayed out of his mouth. "You make a man think you care and then you laugh at him!"

Pulse beating hard in her throat, Sasha assured him, "No one here is laughing at you."

"You need help, man," Nick told him. "I promise I'll get you help."

Lester ignored their reassurances. He jerked Sasha against him and pressed the knife to her throat. "You're coming with me. Time you got what you deserve."

"Lester, let the lady go," Nick ordered firmly. He was now sitting, but he was still looking disoriented.

"I don't take orders from you anymore, Mr. D."

Hand tangled in Sasha's hair, Lester dragged her away from the others, slammed the door and locked it. Then he started into the maze of corridors. Certain that he was going in a different direction than he'd come, she started to panic. Would JoJo and Nick be able to track her? Would Nick even be able to stand without wobbling after she'd clobbered him with that chair?

A series of crashes told her Nick was doing better than just standing.

Suddenly they were in a large clear space and Lester brought them to a stop. "Throw that switch."

Without releasing her hair or removing the knife pressed against her throat, he pointed her toward a support beam holding an electrical box with a lever, even as she heard help coming to her rescue. They were on the rear elevator, the only one that came all the way down into the subbasement. She did as Lester commanded, and the floor beneath them began to move.

"What do you want with me?" Sasha asked him, desperately remembering her training. *Get your attacker talking. Off his guard. Change the script he has planned in his head.*

"You'll see."

"Lester, you're not going to do anything you'll regret, are you?"

"Already done stuff I regret. Couldn't help it. But this time I know what I'm doing. You ruined everything and you gotta pay."

They were passing the upper basement now, on their way to stage level. Sasha imagined she heard Nick shouting her name. She focused on keeping Lester talking.

"What kind of stuff do you regret, Lester? You mean things you did with other women? Mia?"

Lester snapped her head around so she could see him. His expression was feral. She tried not to cringe.

"Mia was a bitch! She broke it off with Mr. D, and then she laughed in my face!"

Heart pounding, Sasha kept a cap on her fear and continued to push. "Is that why you killed her?"

For she was certain he was the one who had murdered Mia Scudella. The mousy maintenance man who kept to the shadows. Who almost no one noticed.

"I had to shut her mouth!" Lester raved. "She was laughing. Calling me names. Telling me I wasn't even a man!" Then he crumpled a bit. Looked haunted by the memory. "I didn't mean to kill her, honest. Didn't mean to kill anyone." Tears squeezed from the mad eyes behind the thick glasses. "Just wanted to shut her up, is all."

Sasha's skin crawled. The poor man was to be pitied, but he was also dangerous. "I'm not laughing at you, Lester."

"You are!"

"I would never laugh at a friend."

The elevator came to a smooth halt.

"Mia tried to make me think we were friends, too."

"I'm not Mia, Lester."

Still guiding her by the hair, he jerked her into the wings of the stage and toward a winding metal staircase that led up to a walkway used by the lighting technicians. What did he mean to do with her up there? It was a long way down to the stage and a fall could be fatal. Or it could leave her with lots of broken bones. Though her heart was in her throat, Sasha knew she had to keep talking, keep trying to get through to him, at least long enough for him to let down his guard.

"I'm *not* Mia," she emphasized as he pushed her up the stairs. "I'm Sasha, remember? JoJo's best friend. You love JoJo, don't you? You tried to protect her from

Mac. She cares about you. I care about you. Let us help you."

"No one can help me now!" he screamed.

But the pressure at her neck let up a bit. She could no longer feel the blade. And the grip on her hair had loosened slightly.

"Sure we can, Lester. I promise. We'll get you—"

"You'll take me away from here and then I'll die!"

"No one's going to take your life."

Poor crazed man would probably be locked up for the rest of his miserable days, though.

As if he knew what she was thinking, he said, "Same thing. Away from here. From the sequins and feathers. Away from all the pretty girls who are nice to me. No one will be nice to me anymore. I might as well be dead."

Was he thinking of committing suicide? Jumping off the bridge? Looking down, she knew that if she didn't get an opening to get away from him first, he would take her with him. They were on the metal walkway now, and she could see the swimmers' tank almost directly below.

"No," she said, trying to impose her will on him. If he thought he should be dead, he wouldn't give a fig about her. "We'll come to see you. JoJo and I. I promise."

She could hear him crying behind her. And below on the stage, a furtive movement caught her eye. Nick peering up from one of the traps. He put a finger to his lips and ducked back down, no doubt to use one of the openings closer to the winding stairs. She felt Lester stiffening and realized he was coming to a crisis point.

Her heart thundered in her chest. It was going to be now or never.

At the same time she went for his knife hand, she stomped on his instep as hard as she could. He screamed and let go of her hair. Hanging onto his wrist, digging her nails in his flesh, she spun around and faced him.

"You lied!" he screamed. "You're not my friend."

Sasha didn't figure reassuring him at this point was going to do her any good. She kicked out, the ball of her foot contacting his shin hard. He jerked in pain and the knife slipped from his fingers. The weapon skittered through the metal grating of the walkway. Seconds later, she heard it clatter to the stage below.

All the fight had gone out of Lester Perkins. He was a broken man. Rivulets of tears drove down his cheeks. His glasses sat crooked, rocking on the tip of his nose like a teeter-totter, and for once, he didn't punch at them. His shoulders were rounded, his hands hung at his sides.

Taking deep breaths, Sasha backed away. Then heard footsteps running across the wing of the stage. She didn't take her gaze from Lester.

She knew the exact moment he decided to end his misery. Defeated, not wanting to be taken away from his sequins and feathers, Lester meant to be part of it forever. The ghost haunting the showroom. He grabbed the rail of the walkway and started to duck under it. And Sasha couldn't let him do it. He was a poor bastard as Nick had said, a slow man, one to be pitied. He hadn't meant to kill Mia. He'd just broken. And he'd tried to save JoJo from Mac in his own sick way.

As he slid his body through the opening, Sasha threw herself onto the walkway and grabbed hold of his belt with both hands, even as he half dangled off the edge.

"Let go!" he demanded.

"No." She couldn't let the sad, misguided and bewildered man fall to his death. "Friends help each other, Lester!" She hooked her legs around a crossbar so he couldn't take her with him. "I promised we would help you."

A weight pounded up the stairs behind her, and JoJo screamed from below, "Hang on! Nick's coming."

"No one can help me," Lester muttered to himself. "Lester's a bad boy. Lock the bad boy in the closet. No more closets for Lester Perkins."

He shoved himself from the walkway, his weight nearly jerking Sasha's arms from their sockets as she hung on with everything she had left.

"Nicky!" she screamed. "Hurry!"

She was doing her best, but light as he was, Lester whipped her upper body over the edge of the walkway. Only her legs were keeping her from falling, too. Her arms burned with the strain. Her upside-down world whirled crazily for a moment . . .

Then Nick was by her side, reaching over the edge, taking the burden of Lester's weight from her. He hauled the maintenance man back up to safety, and Sasha was able to right herself.

Both panting, she and Nick stared at each other, while Lester blubbered between them.

"SO YOU THOUGHT about my offer or what?" Sally Donatelli demanded of his son over dinner the next night. Nick counted to ten silently. "Papa, there's nothing for me to think about. I have my own business to take care of."

"I'm not gonna be around forever."

"Yes, you will. At least long enough to train Caroline to your satisfaction."

His sister's eyes flashed wide. "Nick. I never knew you had such faith in me."

"Caroline is a woman—"

"Who inherited more of your... wiliness ... than either of your two sons." Nick gave his sister a wilting glare. "I know all about the helpful background information you've been distributing about me." JoJo had told him about the package of articles concerning the murders she'd received weeks ago, though he'd never called Caroline on it until now. "That's stopping immediately." Hopefully, if Sasha didn't hate his guts after all that had happened to her, Caroline wouldn't have another candidate to harass. "Understand?"

"What's this?" Sally demanded.

Caroline had the grace to look embarrassed. "I was just trying to save you from another Mia."

"You were trying to prevent me from having outside interests that might keep my attention away from the family." He figured she believed that if she could keep him unattached, there was a chance he'd return to the fold and accept his inheritance—with her as his right hand, of course. "I love you both, but I'm not coming back into the business. *Not ever.*"

"But Nick—"

Nick cut her off. "Caroline's damn smart," he said, turning to his father. "You can trust her judgment when it comes to making money."

"That's what Lucky said."

"You heard from Lucky?" Caroline asked, excitement in her voice.

Sally shrugged. "I had him tracked down."

Nick shook his head. His father would never change, even though Nick had tried doing it for him. While in charge of the business, he'd diversified the family interests, had ventured into legal enterprises, phasing out most, if not all, of what had landed his father in prison in the first place. Sally had been released before he'd finished the transition, and Nick suspected his father hung onto some of the old connections merely as a lure to make him come back and finish the job. Nick wasn't going to fall for the ploy, however.

"You know, Nick, maybe you're right," his father said. "Maybe you should attend to the Caribbean and other, more personal interests, like getting married and having a big family. I'd like to see some little Donatellis before I die."

"Papa, bless your soul, you're never going to die."

"Sasha Brozynski is perfect for you," Sally went on as if Nick hadn't interrupted. "And she's a big, strong *healthy* woman."

Laughing, Nick rose and threw his napkin on the table. "I'm looking for more than a broodmare in a wife." He wanted someone who was loyal, fearless and had a heart as big as...the Grand Canyon. Sasha fit the description, not that he would give his father the satisfaction of knowing that, just yet. "I have to get back."

"We'll continue this conversation next time," his father promised.

Better than hounding him about the business.

Nick only hoped Sasha wanted to see him again. There'd been this awkwardness between them after

Lester had been hauled off by the cops and they'd all gone to the station for the second time that night to give their statements. Sasha hadn't thrown herself into his arms again. She'd clung to JoJo and stared at him in silence as if she were waiting for something. Only he hadn't been sure what she'd wanted to hear. He'd blown it. He'd been dreading the moment he would come face-to-face with her, and, therefore, had been putting it off.

For the first time in his life, Nick felt out of control and was really afraid of something—the possibility of losing the woman he loved.

"So are you going to stay in town or what?" JoJo asked, dressing while Sasha lounged on the bed to keep her company.

"Or what?" Having slept twelve hours after arriving home from the emergency room where she and JoJo had both been checked over, Sasha still felt exhausted. And despondent that she hadn't heard a word from Nick. "I'm not exactly in any physical shape to work at the moment."

Although her injuries were superficial, including the knife wound, Barbie was taking over the rumba for a few nights until everything got straightened out.

"I'm sure Nick would give you some time off to recuperate," JoJo was saying as she dug into her jewelry box.

"Hey, that's your job. I was just filling in."

"I've been thinking about finding a new line of work, anyway. The age thing, you know? And there are always jobs in this town." JoJo studied her worriedly. "You're not avoiding working again...like last time?"

Sasha thought about it. The first attack had changed her life for the worse. She'd avoided getting another gig because she couldn't tolerate the association of being backstage in a theater with what had happened to her. But the physical trauma of the past few days had presented her with an emotional catharsis. She'd fought back, and this time she'd come out on top. The bruises and contusions were temporary. What was important was that her soul was healing.

"I've relearned something I forgot," Sasha told her friend. "Life is taking chances. I'm not afraid to take chances any more."

"Not even with Nick?"

"Well, maybe a little afraid."

JoJo grinned. "A little fear is healthy."

Sasha noticed JoJo was playing with the pearl choker. "Nice pearls. I wore them once."

"I never had the chance to return them to the guy who gave them to me."

"Gaines VanDerZanden."

JoJo's brown eyes widened. "You met?"

"You bet. He tried to get me to spy on Nicky for him."

"You didn't agree?"

"I said I'd think about it."

"Me, too. Now I'm sorry I didn't tell him where he could stuff his pearls. You're not going to do it, are you?"

Sasha sighed. "It took me a while to trust Nicky, but now I do with all my heart. Not that he'll ever believe it."

Having heard the whole story of Sasha and Nick's rocky romance, JoJo insisted, "Hey, he'll cut you some slack."

"I don't know. Trust is pretty important to him." And he hadn't made a move toward her after their tussle with Lester.

"You had good reasons. He'll take that into consideration."

The buzzer startled Sasha as did any unexpected noise these days. She took a big breath and rose. "I'll get it."

"Thanks."

Sasha limped to the front door and was surprised by a delivery person handing her a huge bouquet of Flowers of Paradise. She set the flowers on the table and found a couple of bucks for a tip. JoJo waltzed into the living room as she was pulling out the card.

"From Nicky, I assume?" her friend asked.

Indeed, the exotic blooms *were* from the man she loved, along with the simple missive: *I'm thinking about you.*

WALKING INTO the Caribbean had to be one of the hardest things Sasha had ever done. Not because of what had happened with Mac or Lester, but because she didn't know what might or might not happen with Nick. He was thinking about her. That was promising. Exactly *how* promising she couldn't say.

She was too seasoned to want to be any man's temporary distraction, especially not when it came to a man she loved with her whole heart and soul. But she wasn't certain Nick would want her to be anything more than temporary. He'd made it clear that, while he'd been engaged once, he never intended to make that mistake again.

And considering the dirt Mia had pulled on Nick, who could blame him?

Reminding herself that life was about taking chances, Sasha strode through the casino until she spotted him. He was conferring with Vito. As usual, he was wearing one of his tropical white suits with a red-and-gold shirt that complemented his incredible physique. Her fingers itched to thread themselves through his thick dark hair, to touch his bold, sun-laved features. To feel his body joined with hers once more.

As if he sensed her presence, Nick turned. His emerald green gaze locked with hers and, like the first time she'd seen him, her pulse rushed. He really was drop-dead gorgeous in the best sense of the word.

Nick signaled Vito to go. Then he waited.

Sasha swallowed hard, sashayed toward him, the painkillers she'd taken before leaving JoJo's were working, thank goodness. She'd worn the little gold silk number she'd brought for JoJo's wedding, despite the bruises only half camouflaged by body makeup. As his gaze traveled over every inch of her, and as if the bruises didn't exist, Nick's expression was as appreciative as the first time they'd met.

She stopped close enough to feel his heat. "Need any extra show girls, Nicky?"

"Not extra. Maybe a particular one."

The way he was looking at her, she knew he wasn't talking about another employee any more than she was. Still, she asked, "How about I audition for the spot?"

"Here?"

"Where?"

He crooked his head, moved toward the elevators. Nerves tingling, she followed. A car stood open as if waiting expressly for them. They stepped inside and the doors whooshed closed. She held her breath. He didn't make his move until they were halfway up to the penthouse floor.

Nick hit the stop button as he had the day he'd called her bluff. He trapped her against the wall, hands flattened on either side of her head. Her mouth went dry and she had trouble breathing properly.

"Now what did you really have in mind?" he murmured, his warm breath feathering her face.

"A little prancing," she said innocently.

A dark eyebrow shot up. "I thought you didn't prance."

"Depends on who's doing the asking."

"Okay." Moving back and folding his arms across his chest, he did his best to smother a grin. "So I'm asking."

Trying to breath normally, Sasha circled him in her best show girl fashion, moving smoothly around the perimeter of the elevator, allowing her body to flow and sway. Once again, his gaze on her was so cloying, so potent, that her breasts tightened beneath the silk. Heat crawled up her inner thighs. She felt his hands when he wasn't even touching her.

This time she didn't have to guess at what his lovemaking might be like. She already knew.

Stopping directly in front of Nick, Sasha turned in place. Slowly. He stepped closer, his eyes brushing her breasts. He left only a whisper of room to spare, reached out and ran a thumb lightly along her jawline.

The thrilling sensation quickly spread to every fiber of her body.

"So what do you really want?" he asked.

Taking the biggest chance of her life, she put it all on the line. "You."

"That's easy," he said huskily, his lips drawing closer to tease hers. "You already have me."

"Do I? What part?" That was the important question.

"All of me. Body... heart and soul."

A weight lifted from her spirit and she threw her arms around his neck. "Oh, Nicky, I'm so sorry—"

"I'm sorry—"

Their twin apologies hung lightly between them. The atmosphere, on the other hand, was thick with tension. He looked into her eyes, his gaze filled with love.

"I was brought up to be suspicious of people's motives," he said. "I wasn't prepared for a woman like you."

"I never got the chance to tell you I trusted you, Nicky. I mean, not at first. Maybe a little too late, but—"

Giving her a squeeze, Nick cut her off. "My father thinks I should marry you and have a big family."

Bless Sally's heart. "Do you always do what your father says?"

"Rarely... but this time he's right on the money."

Sasha smiled. "You're willing to gamble on me?"

"I'm smarter than that. I told you before I don't gamble," he said, nibbling at her ear until her flesh responded. "I go for the sure thing. Only..."

She pulled back slightly. "What?"

"Will my family be a problem for you?"

"I like your father. Maybe you can reform him."

"I've been trying for years. What about my sister?"

"Ouch!" Sasha made a squinchy face. "Do I have to like her?"

He nuzzled her forehead. "Think you can tolerate her?"

Sasha sighed. "In small doses."

"Very small doses. I promise," he murmured, nipping at her nose. "You're marrying me, not her."

"Marry? I don't remember a formal proposal."

"Hmm, must'a slipped my mind." He stepped back, took both of her hands in his and solemnly asked, "Will you marry me, Alexandra Brozynski?"

The love she recognized thrilled her more than the words. "You've never called me Alexandra before."

"Stop dodging the question. Will you?"

"Yes, Nicky," Sasha said. "Definitely yes!"

Nick turned her around and his hand hovered over the elevator's Stop button, as if he were about to release it. Hesitating, he asked, "You ever made love in an elevator?"

"No, but I'm open to new experiences."

"Hopefully, *safe* experiences from now on."

"Wherever did you get the idea that *you* were safe?" she demanded, playfully poking him in the chest.

His amused expression becoming intense, Nick pinned her against the wall and kissed her until Sasha believed she no longer had anything to fear...as long as she and Nick could work things out together.

MILLION DOLLAR SWEEPSTAKES (III)

No purchase necessary. To enter, follow the directions published. Method of entry may vary. For eligibility, entries must be received no later than March 31, 1996. No liability is assumed for printing errors, lost, late or misdirected entries. Odds of winning are determined by the number of eligible entries distributed and received. Prizewinners will be determined no later than June 30, 1996.

Sweepstakes open to residents of the U.S. (except Puerto Rico), Canada, Europe and Taiwan who are 18 years of age or older. All applicable laws and regulations apply. Sweepstakes offer void wherever prohibited by law. Values of all prizes are in U.S. currency. This sweepstakes is presented by Torstar Corp., its subsidiaries and affiliates, in conjunction with book, merchandise and/or product offerings. For a copy of the Official Rules send a self-addressed, stamped envelope (WA residents need not affix return postage) to: MILLION DOLLAR SWEEPSTAKES (III) Rules, P.O. Box 4573, Blair, NE 68009, USA.

EXTRA BONUS PRIZE DRAWING

No purchase necessary. The Extra Bonus Prize will be awarded in a random drawing to be conducted no later than 5/30/96 from among all entries received. To qualify, entries must be received by 3/31/96 and comply with published directions. Drawing open to residents of the U.S. (except Puerto Rico), Canada, Europe and Taiwan who are 18 years of age or older. All applicable laws and regulations apply; offer void wherever prohibited by law. Odds of winning are dependent upon number of eligibile entries received. Prize is valued in U.S. currency. The offer is presented by Torstar Corp., its subsidiaries and affiliates in conjunction with book, merchandise and/or product offering. For a copy of the Official Rules governing this sweepstakes, send a self-addressed, stamped envelope (WA residents need not affix return postage) to: Extra Bonus Prize Drawing Rules, P.O. Box 4590, Blair, NE 68009, USA.

SWP-H395

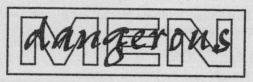

HARLEQUIN®

I N T R I G U E®

**HARLEQUIN INTRIGUE AUTHOR KELSEY ROBERTS
SERVES UP A DOUBLE DOSE OF DANGER AND DESIRE
IN THE EXCITING NEW MINISERIES:**

THE ROSE TATTOO

At the Rose Tattoo, Southern Specialties are served with a
Side Order of Suspense:

On the Menu for June

Dylan Tanner—tall, dark and delectable
Shelby Hunnicott—sweet and sassy
Sizzling Suspense—saucy red herrings with a twist

On the Menu for July

J. D. Porter—hot and spicy
Tory Conway—sinfully rich
Southern Fried Secrets—succulent and juicy

On the Menu for August

Wes Porter—subtly scrumptious
Destiny Talbott—tart and tangy
Mouth-Watering Mystery—deceptively delicious

> Look for Harlequin Intrigue's response to your
> hearty appetite for suspense: THE ROSE TATTOO,
> coming in June, July and August.

HARLEQUIN®

® I N T R I G U E ®

Brush up on your bedside manner with...

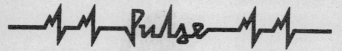

The heart-racing, romantic-suspense trilogy
that's just what the doctor ordered!

In March and April, Harlequin Intrigue brought you
HOT BLOODED and BREATHLESS, the first two books
of a trilogy of medical thrillers by Carly Bishop. Keep
the blood flowing with the last book. It will bring out
the telltale symptoms of reading the best in romance
and mystery.

Don't miss your appointment with:

#323 HEART THROB
by Carly Bishop
May 1995

Available wherever Harlequin books are sold.

HARLEQUIN®

INTRIGUE®

Keep up with Caroline Burnes
and FAMILIAR

You see a black cat walking across the street. It reminds you of something familiar...of course! Familiar, the crime-solving cat, is back for his sixth adventure with Harlequin Intrigue in:

#322 FAMILIAR TALE by Caroline Burnes
May 1995

This time, Familiar is up to his rambunctious kitty rump way down south in Dixie. When children's book author Uncle Eugene is accused of abducting the children he's been charming for years, it's up to Jennifer Barkley, his publicist, and James Tenet, journalist extraordinaire, to find the mischievous munchkins and clear their friend's name before the next story hour!

HARLEQUIN®

Don't miss these Harlequin favorites by some of our most distinguished authors!
And now, you can receive a discount by ordering two or more titles!

HT #25607	PLAIN JANE'S MAN by Kristine Rolofson	$2.99 U.S./$3.50 CAN. ☐
HT #25616	THE BOUNTY HUNTER by Vicki Lewis Thompson	$2.99 U.S./$3.50 CAN. ☐
HP #11674	THE CRUELLEST LIE by Susan Napier	$2.99 U.S./$3.50 CAN. ☐
HP #11699	ISLAND ENCHANTMENT by Robyn Donald	$2.99 U.S./$3.50 CAN. ☐
HR #03268	THE BAD PENNY by Susan Fox	$2.99 ☐
HR #03303	BABY MAKES THREE by Emma Goldrick	$2.99 ☐
HS #70570	REUNITED by Evelyn A. Crowe	$3.50 ☐
HS #70611	ALESSANDRA & THE ARCHANGEL by Judith Arnold	$3.50 U.S./$3.99 CAN. ☐
HI #22291	CRIMSON NIGHTMARE by Patricia Rosemoor	$2.99 U.S./$3.50 CAN. ☐
HAR #16549	THE WEDDING GAMBLE by Muriel Jensen	$3.50 U.S./$3.99 CAN. ☐
HAR #16558	QUINN'S WAY by Rebecca Flanders	$3.50 U.S./$3.99 CAN. ☐
HH #28802	COUNTERFEIT LAIRD by Erin Yorke	$3.99 ☐
HH #28824	A WARRIOR'S WAY by Margaret Moore	$3.99 U.S./$4.50 CAN. ☐

(limited quantities available on certain titles)

	AMOUNT	$
DEDUCT:	**10% DISCOUNT FOR 2+ BOOKS**	$
ADD:	**POSTAGE & HANDLING**	$
	($1.00 for one book, 50¢ for each additional)	
	APPLICABLE TAXES*	$_____
	TOTAL PAYABLE	$_____
	(check or money order—please do not send cash)	

To order, complete this form and send it, along with a check or money order for the total above, payable to Harlequin Books, to: **In the U.S.:** 3010 Walden Avenue, P.O. Box 9047, Buffalo, NY 14269-9047; **in Canada:** P.O. Box 613, Fort Erie, Ontario, L2A 5X3.

Name:_____

Address:_____ City:_____

State/Prov.:_____ Zip/Postal Code:_____

*New York residents remit applicable sales taxes.
Canadian residents remit applicable GST and provincial taxes.

HBACK-AJ2